THE LONG RIDE HOME

THE LONG RIDE HOME

TAWNI WATERS

sourcebooks
fire

Published by Sourcebooks Fire, an imprint of Sourcebooks, Inc.
P.O. Box 4410
Naperville, Illinois 60567-4410
(630) 961-3900
Fax: (630) 961-2168
www.sourcebooks.com

Library of Congress Cataloging-in-Publication data is on file with the publisher.

Printed and bound in the United States of America.
VP 10 9 8 7 6 5 4 3 2 1

For Desi and Tim,
who gave my heart the truest home it has ever known.

ONE

If you picture me as a rugged girl on a Harley, speeding down a leather-black highway at a hundred miles an hour, you might be right. I'm like that some days. A scrawny thing clad in my mom's biker jacket, long blond hair flying behind me in the wind. If you see me riding, you'll think I'm tough. You'll think my biker boots mean I could kick ass if I wanted to, and I guess I could.

What you won't see, though, if you're only glancing at me as I whiz past, is that I have tears on my face. The tears would be frozen if it was winter—really winter, I mean. Alaskan winter. My tears would be almost invisible in Bangkok, lost as they would be in a mist of summer rain.

But I'm in neither of those places, and I'm not riding my Harley just now.

Where I am is in Los-freaking-Angeles, and not the pretty Beverly Hills part either. Horns honk outside my window, and at the other end of our building, neighbors fight, staining the air with verbal graffiti. I lie on my bed, trapped in my head, listening to flies buzz, staring at the water spots on my ceiling.

I shouldn't say "my." The ceiling isn't mine. The ceiling belongs to my mom's lifelong best friend, Mercy, who is appropriately named since she took me in after Mom died. I hated leaving New York behind, but Mom was never very close to her family. I barely knew them. Mercy was the closest thing I had to a caring relative. I love her. Or…I try to. I really loved her before Mom died. Now, every time I see her, I hate her for a second. She's here, and Mom isn't. Why couldn't she be the dead one?

As if to remind me that she is very much alive, Mercy sews in the next room, and the sound of her machine—an old-fashioned one from the seventies—blends with the sounds of the flies, the horns, and the screams, creating an intensely grating brand of music.

I toy with my mom's silver necklace, a nickel-size sun. She got it when she was pregnant with me. It says *Los Milagros* on the back, which is the name of the store she bought it in. She told me the story a million times. When Mom got knocked up, she lived in LA, where she grew up. But when my asshole dad left, she packed up all her shit and drove across the country, trying to feel out a new home. She ended up in New York, but first, she stopped everywhere along the way. In Omaha, she wandered into a jewelry store presided over by a woman she described as "otherworldly," which I had always thought sounded a little cheesy, but whatever. She saw the sun pendant and thought of me.

"No matter what anyone said, I always knew I had to keep you. I knew you were the light of my life," she told me again and again.

She always wore the necklace as a symbol of her love for me, and now I always wear it. Her few possessions that weren't destroyed in the fire are all I have left of her. Her Harley is the biggest thing she left behind. I had it shipped across the country on a truck when I moved to Los Angeles. Now, it's in the shop. It broke down a few months back. "The shop" is a fancy name for my best friend Dean's backyard. When I say "best" friend, I mean "only" friend. You can see that all of my words have double meanings. Sometimes I'll tell you; sometimes I won't. But aren't all people that way?

Mercy's machine whirs on. I cover my ears, hating the sound of it. A fly buzzes in my face, and I swat at it. It evades the blow, soaring triumphantly toward the dusty ceiling fan, which moves sluggishly overhead, providing no relief from the muggy heat. I should probably get up and do something, but what is there to do without my motorcycle? It's not like I have any skills. If I were a writer, I might write a poem, an ugly bit about the ripping noise you hear inside your head when a jagged blade gashes the flesh of your soul wide open. I know "the flesh of your soul" is a strange phrase—oxymoronic, maybe—but I also knew, in that moment I found out Mom was dead, something real inside me tore. I understood then that my soul was a thing of substance, the way maybe she knew when her soul left her body. I felt my soul's twenty-one grams shredding.

Since my tearing, my soul leaks blood at the strangest times. Sometimes, it's at dawn, when birds are chirping outside the window, when the night has given way to pink, and the world is pristine. My life should be a clip from *Snow White,* with me waking up, stretching, and waving daintily at a doe peeking through my window, but instead I'm hearing echoes of that ripping sound, and then I'm bleeding invisibly all over my pillow.

Sometimes, this happens at midnight, though since the tearing, I often sneak into Mercy's liquor cabinet and drink enough gin, vodka, cognac, whatever, to muffle the sound in my head. But some nights, there isn't enough alcohol in the world to drown out that awful noise.

Anyway, enough about that. You must think I'm depressing. If you're not wondering what my name is by now, I feel obliged to inform you that you are afflicted with a tragic lack of natural curiosity. Either that, or I'm boring as fuck, and you don't care about my name, but I'm going to go with option A because option B sucks, at least for me.

Mercy's machine stops whirring.

"Harley," she calls, just in time, because now you know my name. Well, not my real name, but the only name I answer to. I'll save my real name for later because you'll get a kick out of it, and sometimes, you have to keep people waiting to be interesting.

"Yeah?" I say back.

"How about Chinese takeout for dinner? I'm not in the mood for cooking."

"You're never in the mood for cooking." I make it sound like a joke, keeping the spite I feel from tainting my voice. I can't always hold my anger at bay. Some days, I'm a regular rage machine, lashing out at Mercy for the littlest things. She puts up with my bullshit, mostly because she feels sorry for me.

"Touché." She laughs.

I glance at the picture of Mom on my dresser. She's young in that one—I mean really young. She was relatively young when she died, but in the photo, she's my age, which means she's eighteen, give or take. She looks like me, pretty, trying to look tough, wearing the biker jacket that hangs on my bedpost. It was in the car when the house burned down, along with her helmet. *Reinas,* it says on the back, the Spanish word for "queens." The word isn't a decoration. It's an identity. Mom was in a real biker gang. No shit. She would never have called it that though. She called it "the club." They didn't run drugs or anything. Just rode.

"So is Chinese okay?" Mercy calls.

"Sure. Moo goo gai pan for me."

"You got it!"

Twenty minutes later, we're scooping Chinese onto paper plates. Mercy prattles on about some guy she's dating, a leather worker this time. She's had three boyfriends since I moved in, which was six months ago.

"Luke could fix that hole in your jacket," Mercy offers, pulling up the top of her lacy blouse. She has giant boobs, and they're always hanging out. I wish she'd cover those suckers, but she seems to have missed the "What to Wear When You're Over Thirty" article that went around on Facebook. I've thought about tagging her in it, but even I'm not that mean.

"I don't want it fixed," I snap.

"Okay." Mercy smiles, looking at me with wide, accepting eyes. It's a trick Mercy learned in Psychology 101. Apparently, the teacher said that if you wanted information from a person, all you had to do was stay quiet and stare at them benevolently. This was supposed to do two things: make them want to fill the silence and make them want to tell the truth because they felt safe. I know this because Mom used to make fun of Mercy behind her back. "Like we aren't all onto her tricks. Like we didn't all take the same fucking psych class," Mom would say, and we'd laugh. It sounds more sinister than it was. We both found Mercy's quirks endearing.

It might be weird to you that my mom said "fuck" to me or that I'm saying "fuck" to you, for that matter, but that was how it was with me and Mom. It was the two of us. I never met my dad. He was some Salvador Dalí knockoff painter, according to Mom. That's all I know about him besides his name, which I could never forget because it's so ridiculous. Andy Warphol. He's one "p" away from painting vapid pictures of Campbell's soup. He left because he wanted Mom to get an abortion, but she wouldn't. She said she felt me the second I was inside her, like she could sense my soul. "I knew you were the great love of my life," she used to tell me. Mom could be sappy like that.

Instead of getting an abortion, she dropped out of college, moved across the country, and got two jobs. We were pretty poor most of the time. Hell, I was lucky I had more than one pair of shoes. But she loved me, and she was more of a friend than a parent. Say what you want about that shit, but I know a bunch of kids who have parents who refuse to be their friends. I'm pretty sure they would dance if their moms died. But me? Well, you know those pictures they show you in history class of Hiroshima after the atomic bomb? That's what I look like on the inside after losing Mom.

"So how are you doing today?" Mercy asks as she sets her plate on the table, which is compact and trendy, like everything in her apartment.

I shrug and sink into the chair opposite her. "Fine."

"Really?" The way she looks at me then isn't a trick. She cares, and it makes my eyes burn. She reaches out and touches my hand. "Look, kid, I'm here if you need me."

She always calls me kid, like my mom did, and hearing her say it when I'm so close to tears makes me sob outright. So much for tough and distant. Since I've blown my cover, I might as well go for it.

"Sometimes I hear her screaming," I say, gulping. Which is true. Well, mostly true. The "sometimes" part is a lie. Mom screaming is the background music that plays in my head 24–7.

"She didn't feel anything," Mercy comforts. "She was asleep, just like you. One minute dreaming, the next, home." She speaks like "home" is a definitive location, like scientists have a map to the place people go when they die, when the truth is, scientists don't think people go anywhere when they die. There is no home.

I nod, unwilling to divest Mercy of her illusions. If she's trying her silence trick again, it's still not working. We both move rice and chicken around with our forks until she says, "You know that, right? She felt nothing."

I can't tell her what I know, which is this: I have one memory of the fire. Maybe I woke up and passed out again. I don't know. But I remember a few seconds of searing heat and horrifying glow and choking smoke. And screaming. I distinctly heard Mom screaming. And then, she fell silent. And I wonder, did I wake up long enough to hear Mom take her last agonizing breaths?

"You know, right?" Mercy asks me.

I nod again.

Mercy tucks a strand of straight, brown hair behind her ear and smiles. "I ever tell you what your mom said to me the day you were born, right after you slid out, all bloody and messy and squalling?" Mercy was Mom's labor coach. She drove all the way across the country for my birth, and every summer after that, Mom and Mercy somehow managed to see each other for a few weeks. They talked every day.

"No," I say, even though she has. I want to hear it again.

"She said, 'But soft, what light from yonder window breaks? It is the east, and Juliet is the sun.'"

Fuck. I blew my cover. Now you know my real name. It's Juliet. I'm named after—well, you know. Mom was a kick-ass actress. Did I mention that? She was going to UCLA on a scholarship. She gave up all that for me. Ultimately, she gave up her life for me, because if I hadn't been born, that fire wouldn't have started, and Mom would still be alive.

I smile through my tears, tasting snot, which isn't as awesome mixed with moo goo gai pan as you might think. "She said that?" I ask, even though I know she did. I know the story of my birth the way preachers know verses from the Bible.

Mom would smooth my hair away from my face as I rested my head in her lap. "You were screaming so hard," she would say. "And then, the doctor laid you on my belly, and I said, 'Hi, my baby.' You heard my voice, and you stopped crying. I whispered, 'But soft, what light from yonder window breaks?' You looked at me with those pale blue eyes, and I just knew I knew you. It was like coming home."

What Mercy doesn't get is that Mom couldn't die and go home. I was her home. If she isn't with me, and she still exists at all, she's lost. If my dreams are any indication, she's still screaming.

—℮🙟

After dinner, Mercy asks me to watch TV with her. I don't want to, but I do because she seems lonely. Sometimes I wonder who is taking care of whom here. We slouch on Mercy's trendy couch eating chips and watching old episodes of *Friends*. Mercy tells me Mom was in love with Ross, one of the wackiest characters on the show. Her love grew exponentially when he voiced the giraffe in *Madagascar*. She knows

I know this, but neither of us can stop talking about Mom. Mom's not creating any new material, so all we can do is rehash old stories.

As the show drags on, I glance at Mercy's liquor cabinet, willing her to go to bed so I can steal some—whatever. I'm not picky about my alcohol as long as it gets me drunk. It all tastes like shit anyway. Mercy must know I'm stealing it, but she never says anything.

Six episodes in—yeah, we're that pathetic—Mercy finally shuts off the TV and asks, "What do you think you're going to do this summer?"

She acts like I have options. "Well, I was thinking cheer camp," I say sarcastically. This is funny because, suffice it to say that with my "fuck you" attitude and my distinct lack of physical coordination, I'm not a cheer camp kind of girl.

"Ha ha," she quips. "You have your mom's life insurance policy. You could do something fun."

"I doubt Mom would want me to blow her insurance policy on fun."

"Not all of it, but I bet she'd be pissed if you didn't blow some of it."

She's right. Mom was all about carpe diem. Still, I'm not going to give Mercy the satisfaction of agreeing with her. She does that psychology trick, and I think for sure she should be figuring out it doesn't work on me. I imagine having a conversation with Mom about it.

"She tried the psycho-silence-trick on me, like, a hundred times," I'd say.

"Oh my god," Mom would say, then laugh. "What a douchebaget." But she didn't really think Mercy was a douchebaget. Neither of us did. Right now, I kinda think she is though.

Mercy keeps looking at me with those wide, accepting eyes. It works.

"I was thinking I'd take Mom's ashes home," I blurt. I had no idea I was thinking of doing that.

"Like to New York?" Mercy asks.

"Where else?" I didn't know I meant New York until Mercy said it.

"I think that's a beautiful idea," Mercy says.

I'm pretty sure she's going to start in about "the universe" guiding me and "closure" and "magic," so I jump in.

"I was thinking of riding my Harley."

Mercy tries hard to be hip, but this idea is a little too edgy even for her. I see it on her face. Fear is quickly replaced by a less drastic emotion. Mild concern. "Alone? I'm not sure that's safe."

"No, of course not alone. With…"

I *was* thinking of going alone. I mean, in the thirty seconds that have passed since I concocted this plan for my summer, I've only envisioned myself alone. Mercy does her waiting trick again. And for the second time in one night, it works.

"Dean," I blurt. "I was thinking of going with Dean."

Dean who is the only person I know in Los Angeles, besides Mercy. Dean who, when I can't handle school, ditches with me to stare at the ocean. Dean who lets me be quiet as long as I need to and only interrupts my thoughts to say stuff about seeing god in seagulls. Dean who writes poems in this wussy little notebook he keeps in the back pocket of his worn-out jeans. Dean who fixes my motorcycle when it breaks because, in addition to being a poet, he's a motorcycle nut. Dean who is pretty, in a young Elvis meets a young Albert Einstein kind of way. Dean who everyone thinks is gay, probably because he writes poetry. Dean who almost certainly isn't gay because last time we sat on the beach, he kissed me out of nowhere and screwed up our whole friendship for good. Dean who I fucked after he kissed me because I was in a really messed-up headspace, and I needed love, and he felt like love to me just then.

That Dean.

By the time Mercy finally heads to bed, my mind is swimming in Dean. (Note: that's not good.) I open the liquor cabinet, grab a bottle, and take a swig of something clear and bitter—vodka, I think. I don't bother to read the label.

"A shot a day keeps the devil away," I whisper. By devil, I don't mean some scary, red being that haunts a fiery pit at the center of the world. I'm an agnostic who wandered into atheist territory the day the coroner put Mom's ashes in my hands. The only devil I believe in is the monster that lives in my head.

⟞Ꝺ

Mom's urn sits on the mantel in Mercy's apartment. When I say "mantel," I mean "kitchen counter," next to the cookie jar. Mercy's apartment is way too basic for anything as lavish as a real mantel. That double meaning stuff again. I can tell you definitively that you do not want to stumble into Mercy's kitchen at midnight looking for Oreos.

Ever since I told Mercy about my big plan to take Mom's ashes back to New York, I feel nauseous and guilty whenever I look at the urn. I want to forget I ever said so, but it's like I made a promise to Mom.

When I first got the urn, I wasn't ready to scatter the ashes. That would be letting go of the only piece of Mom I had left. Plus, she never told me where she wanted her ashes scattered. Hell, I don't even know if she wanted to be cremated, but after the fire, we had no other option. Still, now that I've had time to clear my head (which means I have gone from perpetually homicidal to frequently suicidally depressed), I'm 100-freaking-percent sure she would not want to spend eternity masquerading as a jar of sugary snacks. Mom was a huge health nut. Maybe, *maybe,* if she were posing as a bowl of hummus, she'd be okay. But cookies? Not a chance.

Meanwhile, as I'm wrestling with the big questions (how should I dispose of my mother's earthly remains?), Dean is probably wrestling with the small ones (why won't the girl I freaked out by sticking my tongue down her throat talk to me?). He keeps calling my cell and leaving messages. It's been more than months since that day at the beach, and he still won't leave me alone. The last one went like this: *Hey, it's Dean.* (Duh. No one else in LA has my number.) *Me again. Look, I'm so sorry. I know I totally messed with your head. I didn't think. I just acted. Which I guess is the problem, right? I didn't expect it to go as far as it did. Hell, I didn't expect it to happen at all. Let me make it up to you. Your Harley is ready to roll. I'll bring it by if that's okay. I pinkie swear I WILL NOT touch you.*

He said "pinkie swear." He does not know this, but he has uttered the proverbial magic words, the syllables that would have gained him entrance to Aladdin's Cave of Wonders if I were the cave in question. My mom and I used to pinkie swear on everything. "It's like signing a contract with the mafia," she'd say. "You can't break it or else." Pinkie swears are deeply imbedded in my psychology. I am powerless in the face of the mighty pinkie swear.

Based solely on his pinkie swear, I call Dean back. It has nothing to do with the fact that I'm rat-in-a-cage bored, ready to gnaw off my leg for entertainment. Nor does it have anything to do with the fact that when I look at his teeth, I want to lick them. Nor does it have anything to do with the fact that my period is more than a month late, and even though I'm trying not to think about it, I do. All the time.

"Harley?" he says when he answers.

My belly flip-flops. Jesus. Does he have to say my name right off? Can't he just say "hello" like a normal person? His voice is deep, which I guess is to be expected, what with him being male and all. He overpronounces his r's, which is not to be expected, and is completely impossible to describe using the written word. The combination makes my heart pound a little faster. His voice is my favorite sound in the world right now, even if I have resisted calling him back for months. Don't give him too much credit, though. Remember my world is populated by flies, my mom's weird friend, and an urn.

"Hey," I say. I'm perched on the edge of one of Mercy's overstuffed chairs, which happens to be this bright turquoise color I'm sure will be horrifyingly unfashionable in about a year. I stare into the kitchen at Mom's ashes.

"Are we okay?" he asks.

I think for a minute. The question seems too big. Is anyone really okay? I finally go with, "Yeah. Of course. I mean, no big deal."

"Thank fucking god," Dean says, and I launch into a theological debate, partially for kicks, but mostly to distract him from the deep conversation about "us" he seems intent on having.

"If there is a god, would he/she appreciate having the adjective 'fucking' attached to his/her name?" I ask.

"Good question," Dean says. "Can I have a few days to mull it over?"

"Certainly." I walk over to the kitchen and run my finger over the ivy leaves engraved along the surface of Mom's urn. I wait for him to talk, but he doesn't. It's like *he's* pulling Mercy's stupid trick, and it works. I'm such a sucker. "So look," I say. "I'm thinking of taking my mom's ashes home."

"To New York?" he asks.

I wonder if he has a transcript of my and Mercy's conversation.

"Where else?" I ask on cue.

"That's cool," he says.

"Only Mercy doesn't want me to go alone," I say.

He doesn't reply, but the silence is pregnant. He's swimming in hope, the nerdy kid frantically raising his hand in the back of the classroom. *Pick me! Pick me!* I pick him. "So you wanna come?"

"Hell, yeah, I do," he says.

I wander back to the living room and plop down in a pretty chair that will be ugly a year from now, feeling like barfing because I'm absolutely sure this trip will change my life forever and not necessarily for the better. And it's not as if my life can really afford any more drastic downgrades. I mean, my period is late, and I'm traveling across the country with my mother's ashes and a guy who scares the shit out of me because I think I might be into him, and I'm really not ready for any emotional commitments right now. One giant life cataclysm is more than I can handle, thank you very much.

Did I say, "Because I might be into him"? I meant, "Because he's a fucking dweeb."

TWO

Six months after my ex-friend Amy's father told her he was dying, we stood beside his coffin. A framed picture of him grinned, poised precariously on the polished mahogany lid. In the photo, he showed off a giant rainbow trout. It was weird how someone could be fishing one year, in a coffin the next.

"I just don't get it," Amy said, staring at the photograph. Her dad looked young in it, way younger than I remembered him. The funeral was over, but Amy and I had stayed behind. She didn't want to be alone with his body. She'd seen what was left of him before they closed the casket. She said it didn't look like her dad.

Before the funeral, she'd whispered jokes to me about his face, which apparently resembled a model from a wax museum. Even then, not having endured the death of a loved one myself, I understood that she was laughing about it to keep herself from falling to pieces. But she wasn't laughing after the funeral. She was borderline catatonic. And wax face or no, she couldn't let her dad get buried without saying goodbye one last time.

She ran her fingers through her short, black hair. "Before he told me he was dying, he made me ants-on-a-log." Ants-on-a-log was her dad's signature dish. He wasn't much of a cook, so celery stalks smeared with peanut butter and covered with raisins were the best he could do. "Then we sat down at the kitchen table like we were going to talk about my gymnastics schedule."

"That so sucks," I said, not knowing what else to say. I'm a good friend when someone goes through something normal, like breaking up or failing a class. But death? That was new for me. That was a year before Mom died. I had no idea I was about to get a crash course.

Amy nodded. "It did suck. Why the hell would he make ants-on-a-log before he told me about his cancer? I mean, 'Hey, kid, I'm kicking the bucket, but here's a nutritious, delicious snack to soften the blow?'"

I still didn't know what to say. "What a dick move" would be what I'd say if we were talking about someone who was alive. But it seemed like an inappropriate eulogy at best. Besides, Amy's dad never made dick moves. He was the coolest dad I'd ever known. I was secretly jealous of Amy, wishing I had a dad like hers. When we were little, he always made us both ants-on-a-log. We liked to pretend the raisins really were ants. We'd imagine we were on *Fear Factor* winning prizes for eating bugs.

I don't guess Amy thought about *Fear Factor* while her dad was telling her about his cancer. Or maybe she did. Who knows?

"Wanna know what I did when he told me he was dying?" Amy asked.

I wasn't sure I did. Entering her pain was hard. Her world had shattered, but mine was still intact. Losing my mom was the worst thing I could conceive of. I didn't want to have to imagine Amy's predicament any more than I had to. Still, I thought I was safe. I mean, what are the odds of two childhood best friends losing a parent? It's the proverbial lightning striking twice.

Amy didn't wait for my response. "I didn't know what to do with the hurricane inside me." She reached out and touched her dad's picture. "So I laughed," she said. "Do I win the 'worst daughter ever' award or what?"

She started to cry, and I put an arm around her broad shoulders. Amy was a big girl, not in a bad way. An Amazon. All the guys thought she was sexy as hell.

"He knows you love him," I said, even though I was pretty sure her dad no longer knew anything.

"You really think so?" she asked.

"Yeah," I lied.

She shrugged, obviously embarrassed about crying though we cried in front of each other all the time. I knew why she was uncomfortable. These tears were different than any tears she'd ever cried. These weren't normal tears. These were end-of-the-world tears. "That's how you know your world has just ended," she said. "You laugh."

She was wrong. A year later, the day after the fire, Mercy sat by my hospital bed and told me Mom didn't make it. I didn't do anything. I was being treated for smoke inhalation, but other than that, I was fine. I regret my silence. I should have laughed like Amy said. Or screamed. Or thrown something. But I simply stared at Mercy, noticing this mole she has on her right shoulder, wondering if it was cancer.

"Do you hear me, Harley?" she asked.

I didn't understand the words. I felt the way I used to feel when Mom and I watched Spanish soap operas together, hearing nothing but nonsense syllables, guessing at the plots.

"What?" I finally asked.

"Honey, your mom died."

Those four words. They run through my head all day, every day. Right now, as I shove jeans in my saddlebag, I hear them. I can't believe I'm doing this. I can't believe I'm going back to New York. I can't believe I'm riding my motorcycle. Most of all, I can't believe I'm going with Dean.

Dean is no Amy, but he's the only friend I've got. I tried to keep in touch with Amy after I came to LA. She was so far away though. How could I explain over the phone what it felt like to lose everything? I mean, at least she still had one parent. I had nothing. So I stopped talking to her about my pain and then, I stopped talking to her altogether. The distance between us grew incrementally, so we barely noticed until it was too late.

Ironically, I understand Amy now better than I ever did when we were friends. I live every day with this crazy hurricane of grief roiling in my belly, just like the one she described when she found out her dad was dying.

Pain is a driver. It drives people to drugs. It drives people crazy. It drove me to the ocean. After I moved to LA, the only one I could imagine understanding my private hurricane was the vast and ever-changing sea. In New York, Mom and I had loved the beach, and now, in LA, the ocean made me feel close to her. I'd go there and stare at the blue-gray sky for hours, picturing the life and death churning beneath the surface of the waves. Sharks eating seals. Sea horses smashing their dainty heads on coral. Cheerful stuff like that.

Dean found me sitting under a dock.

"Hey, you okay?" he asked. He went straight for the jugular. No "Hi, I'm Dean."

He was tall and lanky, blocking out the sun momentarily. His concern made me sob harder. Never cry in front of a nice guy. They go all knight-in-shining-armor on you and shit.

He sat beside me like he'd known me forever. "I can listen if you need an ear," he said.

I looked at him. He had this shoulder-length, wavy brown hair. His eyes, the same gray-blue color as the waves, looked into forever. I totally thought he was seeing what I'd been seeing, sharks eating seals and all that.

"An ear?" I asked. "Are you gonna pull some Van Gogh crap on me?" Did I mention that when I feel vulnerable, I deflect with sarcasm? It's a gift.

"Van Gogh?" he said, and I had to go into the whole story of how Van Gogh sent his ear to a girl to get her attention, which distracted me from my mother's death for a few minutes, which made me forgive him for not knowing the most rudimentary Van Gogh story in the world. Besides, he made up for his lack of Van Gogh knowledge by talking about the Zen of Batman at length, which sounds cheesy when I say it out loud, but somehow it didn't when he said it.

"When he was fighting his way out of that pit," he said, watching a seagull swoop and dive, "it was like busting your way out of the hell inside your head, you know?"

I didn't know what it felt like to climb out of the pit, but I certainly knew what it was like to be in it, having recently been diagnosed with PTSD (thanks, Mom's death), so I nodded.

After that, we started hanging out all the time. He was in his first year of college; I was in my last year of high school. We ditched more classes than we should, enough to earn us both a D, him in biology, me in literature, which was ironic considering how much I loved to read. I'd read every book on the syllabus three times before the class had started, but I simply could not bring myself to write a bullshit paper about Gatsby's love for Daisy and the symbolism of the light burning in the distance. For me, there was no light in the distance. My light in the distance was dead.

Twice, I stole a whole bottle of bourbon from Mercy's cabinet, and Dean and I downed it together, staring out at the waves. Even if I live to be one hundred and have bourbon a thousand times, the taste will always remind me of Dean. The second time we drank together, about halfway through the bottle, he kissed me. It went like this.

He said, "So how do you feel about _____?" (Insert the name of your favorite band here because I can't for the life of me remember which one he actually said. I want to say it was someone cool, maybe a retro band like the Beatles, but I bet it was some epically talentless boy band like Nickelback. We were that drunk.)

I took a swig, making that sexy hacking-wheezing sound I make when taking a shot. I'm not an amateur drinker, but I still can't seem to endure the burn without choking at least a little. My head was swimming. The sea was dancing, which I know the sea does, but the sea was dancing more than usual. So were the clouds. And the cliffs.

"_____? They're my favorite band ever. They rock," I said.

"So do you," he said.

"What?" I asked, taking another drink. (Yes, I tend to be self-destructive. Don't judge me.)

"I said you're the most beautiful girl I've ever known."

Which wasn't what he'd said the first time at all. I was drunk but not that drunk. I was about to say, "No, you didn't," turning the conversation into an argument about semantics instead of a declaration of love, but before I could, he kissed me. Hard. I'd been kissed before, okay? It's not like I was some sweet, innocent girl. But that kiss. Holy shit. It was the way you think kisses are going to be until you finally get kissed and discover kissing isn't as cool as it looks on TV. Dean's kiss was a TV kiss. His kiss made my head explode. Places I didn't even know existed inside me started to buzz.

I pulled away and looked into his eyes, and maybe it was the bourbon, but they were shining, the way people say the tunnel of light shines when you die. Glowing like heaven or some shit like that. Sucking me in.

I'd like to blame what happened next on Dean. I'd like to say he crawled on top of me and not the other way around, but he didn't. I wanted him, and I found myself unzipping his pants for reasons I still can't explain. (Wait, I'll try. Reason number one: bourbon. Reason number two: his shining eyes. Reason number three: the buzzing inside me.) I could say, "Oh, the big, bad boy took advantage of me," but it wasn't that way at all. Dean was the one who said, "Are you sure you want to do this?"

Even though I'd had sex ed, read up on STIs and pregnancy, and learned how to put a condom on a banana, I answered by yanking off my shirt. I didn't even think about protection. I wanted him, and I took him. Contrary to popular opinion, girls do that sometimes.

When we finished, seagulls were screaming, and our clothes were strewn over the rocks. We'd managed to knock over the bottle. What was left of the bourbon was draining into the sand, which was probably for the best. I was pretty sure I was going to have a hellacious hangover the next day. Only then, with the sunset smudging Dean's sweaty skin as he pulled his jeans back on, did I think about the word Mom said to me a million times in all of her talks. "Consequences," she would say. "You are free to do whatever you want, but you are not free to do it without consequences."

If only I'd thought about that the night I lit the scented candle in the hallway because the house smelled bad. If only I'd thought about that as I drifted off to sleep thinking, *I should put out that candle*, and then, *Nah, everything will be fine*.

Mom was right. Everything you do, big or small, has consequences.

THREE

I remember the first time Mom told me about the highway of diamonds. I must have been four or five, and we were taking one of our daily walks, which sounds sweet and inspirational until you find out my mom was a total tyrant when it came to exercise. We'd walk five miles every day, rain or shine, which doesn't seem that bad until you think about the fact that my legs were about as long as soda straws at that point. That was a lot of steps for me, and by the time we were two miles in, I'd be whining and begging to go home. I don't know why I bothered. She never once gave in. Instead, she would sing songs to distract me, one of them being Bob Dylan's "A Hard Rain's A-Gonna Fall."

In spite of my best efforts to maintain my displeasure at being forced to walk, I'd lose myself in the song's heartbreaking lyrics and melody.

"What's it about, Momma?" I asked, knowing it made me want to cry but not understanding why.

"It's about a little boy who has left his father on a long trip. When he sees his daddy again, he tells him all the things he's seen."

She sang again, and I thought the kid must have had a really weird trip from his descriptions. The lyric that always made me wonder the most was about a highway of diamonds. It felt magical to me, like something from *The Chronicles of Narnia* that Mom read to me some nights. So I asked her about it.

Mom thought for a minute, and then pointed to the sidewalk in front of our feet, shimmering in the sun. "See how the sidewalk looks like it's filled with diamonds if you look right in front of you?"

"Yeah," I said, my tiny rib cage swelling with wonder.

"But if you look far away, you can't see the diamonds anymore?"

She was right. You couldn't. "Uh-huh."

"Well, I think the song means to trust you will be taken care of. You take the next step in front of you, the one that shines, the one that seems right, and then, you take the next one and the next, and before you know it, you're home."

I jumped from one glittering patch of sidewalk to the next that day. I forgot to complain, and Mom was right. Before I knew it, we were home.

I remembered that conversation when Dean and I packed up the bike for our trip this morning, and now, as I steer around a sharp bend, I notice the highway glittering a few feet in front of us. As a tribute to Mom, I decide to take one glittering step after the next until finally, hopefully (dear god in heaven, *please*?), I'm home.

"You doing okay?" Dean screams in my ear.

I can barely hear him over the wind.

"Awesome!" I yell back.

The wind burns my face. The sun melts my scalp through my helmet. The roaring of the engine drowns out all other sounds, but still, I'd be lying if I told you Dean's arms around my waist aren't what I notice most. A lot of guys would have a problem riding on the back of some chick's bike, but not Dean. He doesn't give a shit what people think.

The road stretches forever, and if there is a heaven, I hope it looks like this—a big blur of blue and green, bisected by a hazy, gray line of horizon.

There are a few things in this world I can say I have truly loved. One is my mom. One is my dog Leroy Brown, who got run over when I was in fourth grade. And one is the open road.

Dean's heat seeps through my leather jacket, and all I can do is wonder what I will have to give up if I give in to him. What will having a boyfriend do to my life? Will I need to stop riding my Harley alone? I mean having him here now is cool, but having him along all the time? No way. Will I have to sacrifice one of the only things I have ever truly loved, the only one I have left?

We pull over at a rest stop. As I yank off my helmet, Dean whoops. "What a rush!"

I laugh. "Heel, Cujo. You're getting a little crazy."

He grins, and it does me in, makes my belly flip-flop sixteen different ways. I hate that he has that kind of power over me.

"Want something to drink?" He pulls off his helmet.

"Nah, I'm good," I say, even though I'm not good at all. I hate charity. I'll buy my own damn drink.

He strides to the snack machines, and I go to the bathroom. My stomach hurts as I walk inside the stall. I hope it's cramps, but it's probably not. It's probably sheer terror. "Let there be blood," I whisper again and again like a mantra. Closing my eyes and praying to a god I'm almost sure I don't believe in, I yank down my pants and sink onto the toilet. I barely dare to look, but I do. My panties are clean. Shit.

I'm not crazy-town late, okay? Only a few weeks. It could be anything. Hormones. Stress. Motherfucking stress for sure. I mean, Jesus Christ, my mother died. Of course I'm stressed. I knew this one girl who stopped having her period for six months after her family got evicted. True story.

I pee and yank my pants back up, resisting the urging of the little voice inside my head that tells me I need to buy a pregnancy test. *Come on. I'm a few weeks late. Don't be so dramatic,* I retort. Yes, I talk to voices in my head. And yes, I lie to them about how late my period is. No, that doesn't make me crazy. I don't think.

When I walk outside, Dean's wearing headphones and gazing up at the sky, occasionally bopping to whatever music he's listening to. I don't know if "bopping" is actually the word for what he's doing. It sounds clumsy, and he's anything but. He's barely moving, but he's still graceful. I wish I could dance like that. I take him in like he is art, noting his lean lines and wiry contours, admiring the way his curls fall over the brown of his skin. Smiling, he sways his hips slightly, like he's with an invisible and very desired partner. Wishing it were me, I go to him. "Hey," I say, placing my hand on the small of his back since he probably can't hear me.

He spins toward me and grabs my hand, starting to do this little jig. "Dance with me, Harley," he says too loud.

"No way." I pull away. "I don't dance."

He yanks the headphones out of his phone so that I can hear the music, some Irish-sounding rock. The lead singer has a brogue, and there are bagpipes involved. "Come on!" he says, reaching for my hand again.

I panic. Did I mention that I'm terrified of dancing? When I was little, the kids in PE laughed at me for being a klutz, and I guess I believed them. The thought of moving in front of people chills me. Mom's insistence that I take karate for self-defense was the source of almost every fight we ever had. And Mercy's frequent, well-intentioned pleas that I join her for yoga have been the cause of more than one almost panic attack. As a rule, I steer the fuck clear of sports, dancing, and anything else that requires coordination.

"I said no!" I snap, sounding nastier than I mean to.

He stops dancing. "Whoa, sorry. You really *don't* want to dance."

"Isn't that what I said?"

Dean lies in the grass, threading his hands behind his head. I feel like I should say I'm sorry, but he seems okay, so I go the vending machine instead and buy a Sprite.

"I thought you said you weren't thirsty," he calls.

"I changed my mind." I throw the Sprite back in a few gulps, toss the empty bottle in the trash can, and wipe my mouth with the back of my hand.

"Join me?" He glances at the place beside him. I almost say no, but I already feel bad about not dancing with him. Instead, I walk over and lie next to him. I'm acutely aware of his breathing, so much so that I find myself synchronizing my breaths with his.

When I was a kid, Mom took me to church a few times. She said she didn't personally dig organized religion, but she wanted me to know my options. I remember watching this puppet show about the devil tempting a good little girl to do bad things. He was red with horns and not cute at all. I had no idea my own personal tempter would look like Dean. He's like candy in human form. It's hard to keep my tongue off him.

"What do you see?" I ask because I can't think of anything else to say.

"What?" he asks.

"The cloud game, dumb ass. What do the clouds look like to you?"

He smiles. His teeth are ridiculously white. His canines stick out a little, which makes his smile almost perfect, which is infinitely sexier than totally perfect. Did I mention I have a thing for mouths?

"Oh, okay." He laughs. "An ice-skating rhino?"

"An ice-skating rhino?" I scoff. "Where? I don't see a rhino."

"Isn't this game supposed to be about imagination? Anything goes? There are no wrong answers?"

"Well, there were no wrong answers until you said, 'Ice-skating rhino.' Now, there are wrong answers."

He points at a cloud. "See the horn?"

I squint. "I'll give you a triceratops. No way it's a rhino."

"What's the difference? They both have horns." Dean sounds a little exasperated, flirtatiously so, like this conversation might turn into a tickle fight if I'm not careful.

"The difference is one has been extinct for millions of years. You can visit the other at the San Diego Zoo on a Tuesday morning."

"What does that have to do with cloud shapes?" Dean asks. "I feel like you're getting tangential to distract from the real debate."

"I feel like you're using words like 'tangential' to impress me."

"Are you impressed?"

"Not a fucking chance, Rhino Boy." I resist the urge to kiss him and punch him in the arm instead. "You ready?" I stand and dust the grass from my jeans.

"Ready," he says, doing the same.

As we walk back to the bike, a woman passes. She has hair like my mom's, straight and long. She walks the same, a certain delicacy to her steps. It's stupid, but for one moment, I think it might really be her. I actually make the "m" sound in the word "mom" before I bite my tongue, reminding myself that Mom is now a jar of ashes tucked into my saddlebag.

"You okay?" Dean looks at me, concerned. I hate the way he seems to sense every shift in the weather patterns of my mind. He's like motherfucking Santa. He sees you when you're sleeping. He knows when you're awake.

"I'm cool." I shrug. "I think I swallowed a bug."

"Protein," Dean says.

I'd usually be all over that joke, but I'm so distracted by the mom-woman, who up close looks nothing like her, that I miss it completely. "Yeah." I nod.

"You actually think I'm serious?" he asks.

"About what?"

"You think I think gnats are a viable source of protein?"

I watch the woman disappear into the restroom. It almost makes me cry, but then it makes me laugh, because I think some crap about Mom having gone off the eternal public restroom in the sky. Hey, it's as believable as any other theory I've heard. "It wouldn't be the weirdest thing you've ever thought," I say.

Dean threads his fingers through mine. He pinkie swore he wouldn't touch me. I glance at my phone to check the time. We've been on the road for exactly two hours and thirty-six minutes, and he's already broken his promise. Still, I cannot bring myself to tell him to let go.

"You know breaking a pinkie swear is like breaking a promise to the mafia?" I say.

"So are you going to send someone to bust my kneecaps?"

"Nah, I'll do it myself."

When he slides his hand out of mine to put on his helmet, my fingers go cold.

"I'm not surprised you don't hire people to bust kneecaps. You strike me as the kind of girl who does her own dirty work," he says, climbing on the motorcycle.

"What makes you think that?" I fasten my helmet strap and stare at him menacingly until he gets the hint and scoots back. If he thinks I'm letting him drive, he's nuts.

"I was with you on that beach, remember?" he says.

I climb on and start the engine. "You promised to never mention that again!" I yell.

As I pull out onto the highway, he stays quiet. I'm not sure if he actually didn't hear me or if he's being his usual bullheaded self.

We ride until the sun falls over the edge of the horizon and starts to disappear in a blaze of purple. We pull over at a deserted campground. Twenty dollars for the night, and it even has showers. Not a bad deal as far as lodgings go.

"If bugs are a good source of protein, I'm in luck because I'm pretty sure I have a few imbedded between my teeth," I say as I shut down the engine. I'm 100 percent determined not to let the last topic we discussed be the one that opens our conversation now.

"Let's see," Dean says, undoing his helmet.

I smile for him, chimpanzee style.

He comes in close enough that I can feel his breath burning my face. "Ew," he says. "Yep. Either that's a green beetle wing, or you have some lettuce left over from lunch. Not sure which."

I run my tongue over my teeth self-consciously.

"Totally kidding," he says. "Are you sure you don't have Asperger's?"

"What the hell kind of question is that?" I hang my helmet on the handlebars. The helmet used to be Mom's. It has her name painted on the back. *Mary*.

"You're kinda a classic case. People with Asperger's are brilliant and utterly amazing but don't always get when people are joking."

"You're a dick," I say.

"What?" he says. "I'd still adore you if you had Asperger's. In fact, I'd think you were even cooler than I already do. People with Asperger's are the next step in the evolution of the human race."

"Yeah?" I say, rustling around in the saddlebag. "Well, I hate to disappoint you, but I'm not the missing link." I toss the ultra-compact tent I bought for the trip on the ground. "Pitch that, Science Boy."

"I thought I was Rhino Boy." He unwraps the tent.

"Same difference." I pull out the two sleeping bags, also ultra-compact.

"Not really," Dean says. "If you stuck with one pet name, it would start to feel like affection. Right now, your nicknames just feel like mockery."

"That's how they're supposed to feel." I toss his sleeping bag, which rolled up is about the size of a soccer ball, his way. It hits him in the gut.

"Thanks." Dean rubs his stomach, feigning injury. It's altogether unconvincing. "And I didn't say you were the missing link. I said you were the next step in human evolution. The missing link is the last step not the next step."

"Do you ever shut up?"

"Not unless I'm sleeping."

I bustle around setting up camp, trying not to notice Dean. My thighs and ass are sore, but it's a good hurt, the kind I imagine cowboys used to feel after rustling cattle or whatever the hell it is they did. Night is just starting to fall, and moonlight drifts through the branches, making webs of light on the ground. We have driven only one afternoon, but we are worlds away from the ocean. The landscape is mostly red dirt and scrub oaks and rocks. I worry about rattlesnakes crawling into my sleeping bag. I will definitely make Dean be the one to sleep outside the tent. I hate to go all damsel in distress on him. I'm a feminist, after all, just like my mother before me. Still, once in a while, I've been known to fall back on traditional gender roles. Usually when spiders need to be smooshed.

"You hungry?" Dean asks.

"I could eat a rhino," I say. "Or a triceratops. There's really no difference."

He smiles, ripping open a bag of beef jerky. "I'm pretty sure this is one of the two." He holds out the jerky. I bury my hand in the bag.

After dinner, which consists of jerky, apples, and a healthy dose of water, we sit by the fire pit while Dean plays his ukulele. There is no fire, just a pit, because it's so hot we can barely breathe as it is. Overhead, the moon hangs blue.

"What made you decide to play the ukulele?" I ask as he mindlessly strums.

"I wanted to pick up chicks," he says.

"Good call," I say. "I've yet to meet a woman who can resist the allure of a man holding a ukulele." I glance at him sideways. He's got that glow about him that people get when they are outside on a moonlit night. He looks otherworldly.

He nods. "So I've discovered."

Suddenly, I'm picturing Dean with thousands of ukulele-hungry groupies hanging off him, and I'm jealous. It's stupid, I know, but I feel a little sick. "So how many girls have you lured to your lair?" I try to sound casual when I say it, staring up at the sky like his answer is no big deal to me. The stars pulse, sending out an SOS.

"What?" he asks. He must not believe my "this isn't an important conversation" act because he stops strumming.

"How many?" I ask again.

"How many girls have I been with?" he asks.

I nod. Crickets chirp, and somewhere in the distance, something hoots. Thank god. I have inadvertently wandered into "conversation about us" territory and am desperate for a distraction. "Is that an owl?" I ask.

Dean doesn't seem to hear the question. "One," he says. "I've been with one person. She was the prettiest girl in the world."

It is so quiet between us, I finally feel obligated to blurt out, "Me too," even though it's not true, even though I've been with one other person besides Dean. Now doesn't seem like the right time to go all scout's honor on him.

"You really think I'm the prettiest girl in the world?" Dean asks.

I try not to show him how much what he said means to me. No one else has ever thought I was the prettiest girl in the world. Except Mom. She always told me that.

"Second only to Marilyn Monroe," I answer.

He laughs, then starts to play a Neil Young song my mom loved about a woman riding a Harley on a desert highway. It's called "Unknown Legend."

He's probably thinking about me when he sings, but my mom is the only unknown legend I've met. I see my mom riding down the dark desert highway, forever and ever. I hope she really is flying, happy, free, wild, the way she was in life. Unexpectedly, a wave of grief washes over me and almost knocks me flat. I've been this way since Mom died. One second, I'm fine. The next, I'm almost doubled over with pain, trying to keep from bursting into tears for no apparent reason. I clench my fists, wishing Mercy's liquor cabinet was nearby. Why didn't I think to steal a bottle for the road? I have nothing to numb the pain.

The tearing sound in my brain starts, and then, I hear Mom screaming. After that, it's Mercy saying, "Honey, your mom died." My heart pounds against my rib cage like an ape trying to break out of a zoo. I can't breathe.

Shit. It's happening again.

This is probably as good a time as any to tell you that in the month after Mom died, I had two full-blown panic attacks. The second one was so bad, Mercy rushed me to the hospital. We were both certain I was dying. I wasn't, but I'm pretty sure it was just as scary as real death. The doctor gave me a pamphlet about grief counseling and a prescription for clonazepam, which I took for two days and never touched again. Mom always said psychiatric meds were dangerous. I looked up clonazepam on the internet, and it turned out she was right. Clonazepam caused all kinds of horrible side effects, including but not limited to addiction, seizures, and death. Thanks, but no thanks, asshats. Maybe the medication helps some people, but I already had all I could handle.

I *am* fine. *It's only a panic attack,* I remind myself. Staring at the stars, I repeat the mantra the doctors gave me for dealing with this shit. *It's. Only. A. Panic. Attack.*

So far, since I went to the hospital, the mantra has helped every time I started to panic. It's working now. My heartbeat slows. I count five physical things to ground myself, the way the doctors said I should. A tree trunk. A rock. A clump of grass. An ugly black bug. Dean. Thinking of Dean is what finally makes my breathing go back to normal. I reach for his hand and stop his fingers from moving along the ukulele strings.

"You okay?" he asks.

I think about telling him what I'm feeling, but that makes my breathing go ragged again, so instead I say, "I'm fine." He leans in and kisses me. His lips are soft and warm. My heartbeat speeds up, this time for completely different reasons.

After a couple of minutes, Dean slides his hand under my shirt, running his fingers along my belly. I pull away. "If you think buttering me up is going to make me let you sleep in the tent, you've got another thing coming. I am so not sleeping out here with the rattlesnakes."

"We could both sleep in the tent," he offers.

"Dream on, Ukulele Boy."

"You sure?" he asks.

I nod.

"You're the boss." Smiling, he resumes his strumming.

⟡

I wake up to the sound of birds. As my dreams evaporate, I think I'm home with Mom, curled up in my queen-size bed with pink ruffles. (My bedroom looked like someone ate a bunch of cotton candy and threw up everywhere. Don't judge me. Mom decorated when I was twelve and going through my princess phase.) A crow caws, and I remember Mom's dead. "Quoth the raven, 'Nevermore,'" I mutter, even though it isn't a raven, and quoting Edgar Allan Poe before you open your eyes has to be really bad juju. I believe I'm at Mercy's house until the rock digging into my spine reminds me I'm not in a bed at all. I open my eyes and watch the sunlight filter through the flimsy fabric of the tent.

"Dean?" I call. No answer. "Dean?" I yank on a sweatshirt and stumble outside.

Dean's nowhere to be found, but his sleeping bag is still

unrolled by the fire pit. A cup of gas station coffee sits on a stump he apparently used for a bedside table, judging from the opened copy of the *New Yorker* that rests there. What kind of college freshman reads the *New Yorker*? He's so pretentious.

I pick up the coffee and find a note scribbled on a napkin underneath it: *Rise and shine, morning glory. Thought you could use a pick-me-up. Your tent got pretty crazy last night. What were you doing in there, wrestling bears? P.S. Do you always snore like that?*

I blush and am grateful no one is around to see it. I have always been what Mom liked to call an "active sleeper," meaning I talk, walk, and sometimes pee in my sleep. Not in my pants, mind you. Traditionally, I get up and find a completely inappropriate place to relieve my bladder, usually the hamper or a potted plant. The inappropriate peeing has happened only a few times in my life, but it's enough to make me phobic about sleeping near anyone I don't know well. As I stare at Dean's chicken-scratch handwriting, I find myself asking the million-dollar question: Did I or did I not pee in Dean's sleeping bag last night? You think I'm being facetious. I'm not. Once, I peed on Mom's pillow.

I pick up the coffee and take a sip. Predictably, it tastes like shit. "Dean?" I call again. Still no answer. I wander into a cluster of scrub oaks. My pants are around my ankles before I remember to hope for a spot of red in my panties. There is no blood, and judging from the sheer volume of urine I expel, I am almost sure I did not sleep-pee last night. I return to the stump, pick up Dean's note, and stare at it. *Rise and shine, morning glory.* My mom used to wake me up with those words. I thought she was the only person in the world who said that. How the hell did he know? For a second, I believe in an afterlife, that Mom is watching from a cloud somewhere, sending psychic messages to Dean, telling him what to say to make her daughter trust him. What if Mom is trying to set me up with Dean? That would be just like her. She was such a control freak. If there was any way she could stick around after death to orchestrate my love life, she'd totally do it.

"Mom, what the hell are you up to?" I say.

"She wrestles bears in her sleep *and* talks to herself," Dean says behind me.

I jump and dump a little coffee on my hand, which burns me, which in turn makes me whirl around and slap the shit out of Dean's arm.

"Whoa!" He laughs, rubbing his bicep. "Did I startle you?"

"You scared the hell out of me!" I try not to let on that the sight of him sporting sexy bed-head and five o'clock shadow makes me long for that moment on the beach.

Remember that growling noise he made when his mouth was right by your ear? I think.

No, I answer myself. (He's right. I do talk to myself, but usually inside my head.) *I don't remember that at all.*

Of course, I'm lying. I remember it very well.

"Where were you?" I ask.

He points at my coffee, as if that should be an answer.

"I mean after you got the coffee, Stephen Hawking. Clearly, you got coffee and then went somewhere else."

"Can't a guy take a piss without enduring the inquisition upon his return? And you're welcome for the coffee."

He seems mildly hurt, and I am instantly remorseful. "Thank you for the coffee." Before I can stop myself, I kiss his cheek. The smell of his skin takes me right back to that beach. Which is the last place I need to be. I pull away and take a huge swig of my hellacious coffee.

My kiss seems to have worked magic on Dean. His eyes have gone from wounded to elated in two seconds flat. "How's the coffee?" he asks.

I smile sweetly. "It tastes like vomit."

"Really? That bad?"

I nod. "It's bringing back when I rode the Tilt-A-Whirl three times at an amusement park."

"Nothing like a cup of barf in the morning," he says, stretching.

(Yes, his shirt does ride up and reveal the line of hair on his belly. No, I don't notice.)

As we break down our camp together, I'm keenly aware of his biceps. I feel like some loser heroine in a romance novel. If I'm not careful, I'll be gushing about manhoods and heaving bosoms in no time.

Before you decide I'm some simpering girl who got all twitterpated when *Twilight* came out, let me explain. Mom was uncharacteristically sketchy when it came to having "the talk" with me. I'm happy to announce that she grew out of her "squeamish about sex" phase, and by the time I was seventeen and lost my virginity to a notorious womanizer, she was there to mop up my tears and listen to the whole sordid story. (Actually, it was a short story—thirty seconds, give or take.)

But when puberty hit me in sixth grade, she was visibly daunted. She gave me a book called *Your Beautiful Body* full of labeled, anatomically correct cartoons. *Meet your beautiful vagina,* one said. The vagina in question was not beautiful, but in its defense, I have never seen a beautiful vagina, cartoon or otherwise. Not that I've seen many, but the ones I have seen looked like aliens. Ditto for penises. Who decided sex organs were sexy? They are so not. When I finished the book, I was 100 percent sure sex happened when an animated sperm with googly eyes and an animated egg with puckered lips loved each other very much. Any other girl my age would have cleared up her confusion by breaking into her dad's porn stash or running questionable internet searches, but since I didn't have a dad, and our only computer was in Mom's bedroom, I did the next best thing, which was break into Mom's romance novel stash. They were completely outdated. I think she must have stolen them from *her* mom. Still, I got the gist of how actual sex happened from those books, but I think I will always be prone to referring to my lady parts as my "delicate flower."

I watch Dean shove the tent into its bag. Imagining us on the beach, I silently narrate the memory. *Aching, she pulled him to her and held his head against her breasts, relishing the sensation of his hair tickling her skin. "Take me, you beast," she said, gasping.*

I threw in the "Take me, you beast" for effect. I did not actually say, "Take me, you beast." Our dialogue went something like this:

Dean: "Are you sure?"

Me: "Hell yeah, I'm sure."

And then, in '70s romance novel speak, we succumbed to our burning desire. I remember when it was over, looking at the sunset, smelling Dean's skin, and feeling warmth washing my insides, warmth that at the time felt like love. Of course, in retrospect it was the hormones talking. Mom's cartoon sex book taught me that much.

When we are all packed up, Dean asks, "You driving or am I?"

"I am," I say without hesitation. I always drive. If Dean doesn't know that by now, he's just plain stupid.

FOUR

Again, I wish I could say that Dean's hands on my waist don't affect me, but they still do. More than yesterday, if I'm honest with myself. Even when the landscape is at its most breathtaking, I'm hyperfocused on his fingers webbing my belly button. Red rocks tower above us, slicing the sky with their jagged edges, turning the landscape into a scene from a cowboy movie. His torso pressed against my back is warm, and even in the desert heat, it's soothing, like hot soup on a rainy day. Like home. He makes me feel safe, and that's the problem. Nothing scares me more than feeling safe. I felt safe with Mom, and look how that ended. If it had ever occurred to me that Mom might leave someday, maybe I wouldn't have let myself get so attached. Maybe I would have kept a little piece of my heart for me, but my DNA is all twisted up with hers, and since she is now nothing but ash in my saddlebag, I'm ash too.

We drive for hours, stopping every once in a while to pee. Every time we stop, I say a prayer to the period gods. They do not deign to hear my supplications. By pit stop number three, a McDonald's this time, I'm pretty panicked as I pull up my jeans. Maybe because the sperm donor for my maybe-baby is with me, I can't push the lateness of my period out of my head. It occurs to me for the first time this might be more than a pregnancy scare. This might be a pregnancy. I remember the cartoon zygote from Mom's sex book and imagine one growing inside me. That scares the living shit out of me. Zygotes don't stay zygotes. Zygotes turn into embryos. Hell, it's an embryo already. And embryos turn into fetuses, and fetuses turn into babies. Babies poop and cry and need things I can't even begin to imagine. Like fathers. Babies need fathers. If I had a father, I wouldn't be in the mess I'm in now, crashing in Mom's friend's guest room, pretending to have a home. I lean my head against the cool metal wall of the bathroom stall and cry, never mind the germs. However, I pull myself together quickly, blow my nose, and open the stall door. In the mirror, my face is red, taut. I look I've been crying. Hell, I look like I've been dying. I look like a walking corpse.

After dropping some Visine into my eyes and smearing on some lip gloss, I stroll into the dining area of the McDonald's. Dean stares at the menu.

"Hey." I force a smile I don't feel.

"Hey, back," he says.

"You're not seriously thinking of ordering fast food,

are you?" I ask. Mom was not traditionally religious, but she was zealous about some things. Healthy food was one of them.

"Well, I was—" Dean says.

"You'd be better off eating dog food. Have you seen what goes into the chicken nuggets?"

"I was going to order a cheeseburger."

"Their cheeseburgers don't decay. You can sit one on a shelf for a year, and it will still look exactly the same as the day you bought it." I can hear my voice rising. I know the rage I feel is irrational, but I can't seem to control it. These days, I'm pissed off for no good reason a lot.

Dean shrugs. "Cool."

"Cool? I think you mean disgusting."

"No, actually, I mean 'cool,'" Dean insists.

"Jesus, Dean."

"You're the second girl to call me Jesus. The first one was in the bedroom." Dean smiles when he says this. I know it's a joke. Still, jealousy twists my insides.

"I thought you said I was your first."

"Harley, get a grip. I was kidding. You *were* the first."

I burst into tears. (When I got diagnosed with PTSD, the doctor warned me about the crying, but I had no idea how bad it would get.)

Looking baffled, Dean puts an arm around my shoulder and leads me away from the counter. "Okay, Harley, I'm sorry, but I don't understand what's going on here. Fill me in. Are you crying because I'm ordering a cheeseburger, because I have a Christ complex, or because I made a joke about another girl?"

I don't know what to say. I'm keenly aware I'm acting like a freak. I'm crying because I might be pregnant, but I can't bring myself to tell him that, so I play my ace. "I'm crying because my mom is dead."

It works. "Oh, man," Dean says. "I'm so sorry, Harley." He wraps his arms around me, and for a second, I feel safe. I forget to be afraid. I bury my face in his shoulder and breathe that salty-sweet smell of his. Suddenly, I *am* crying because Mom is dead. It's like that scene at the end of *Braveheart*, the one where they cut out his guts while he's still alive. I've felt like that ever since Mercy said, "Honey, your mom died."

Dean kisses the top of my head. "Look, Harley. I know I will never be able to totally get what you're feeling. I've never had to go through what you're going through. But if you need to cry and wipe your snot on someone, I'm your guy."

How does he always know exactly the right thing to say?

"Thanks," I whisper.

"Seriously, if I can do anything for you, tell me."

"You can get me a fucking cheeseburger," I say, pulling away from him and swiping at my nose with the back of my hand.

Dean laughs. "Are you serious? I thought they were carcinogenic or something."

I smile through my tears. "They are, and I want one. It's high time I start killing myself slowly like a good American girl."

Dean leans in and kisses me on the forehead. His lips

are warm and wet. That pain in my belly intensifies, but it's different now. It's a good kind of hurt. "You are the most bewildering, adorable creature I have ever known," he says.

"That would have been sweet if you didn't use the word 'creature' to describe me," I deflect.

Dean laughs. "Sorry. I meant to say you were the most adorable organism I'd ever known. Now go sit down, Creature Feature, and I'll get you that fucking cheeseburger."

I choose a booth in the corner and watch a little girl with lopsided braids playing in the ball pit. "Mommy, I'm swimming!" she shouts, neck deep in plastic balls, clumsily practicing her breaststroke. My eyes get hot again. I close them to keep tears from falling. I've already melted down twice in this particular fast-food joint, and I'd rather not go for a third.

"Watch out for sharks!" a woman's voice says, and the little girl squeals. Inside my head, I'm four again and at the beach with Mom. The sun is dropping into the sea, turning it oxblood red. My face is pressed against her shoulder, and she whispers, "'But soft, what light from yonder window breaks? It is the east, and Juliet is the sun.'" The waves roll in and out.

"Your fucking cheeseburger, milady." Dean's voice snaps me out of my memory.

I open my eyes as he sets a food-laden tray on the table. I poke at the paper-wrapped hockey puck masquerading as a burger. "Do I dare?" I ask.

"You'd better dare." Dean slides into the booth beside me. "I spent my life savings on this baby. Got you fries too." He steals a fry and shoves it in his mouth.

Slowly, I unwrap the burger, trying not to picture that story that went around online, the one about how McDonald's cheeseburgers don't decay. "You know this isn't actually edible, right?" I say. And then I take a bite.

"Edible means 'able to be eaten.' You're eating it right now, so clearly, it's edible."

Glaring, I think about busting out my iPhone and giving him the dictionary.com definition of "edible," which I am sure will say something like, "able to be eaten without causing cancer, death, or both," but the cheeseburger is too damn good. I don't want to put it down. As I chew, Dean watches me eagerly. "Who are you, fucking Sam I Am?" I say after I swallow.

"Am I who?" Dean asks.

"You know, Sam I Am, from the children's book? Sam I Am chases the yellow dude around, forcing green eggs and ham down his throat, asking everyone if they like green eggs and ham?'"

"In my defense, I really didn't force anything down your throat," Dean says. "You asked me to buy you the cheeseburger."

"Well, you're staring at me, like you're dying to find out what I think."

"I can't lie. I *am* dying to find out." Dean steals another fry.

I plop the burger on the tray. "It's terrible."

Dean looks so disappointed, I decide to tell the truth. "I'm kidding. This burger is the shit." I pick it up and take another bite. But it doesn't keep me from reciting Dr. Seuss to him or remembering why I have that book memorized. I can still hear Mom squealing gleefully while she read to me, using different voices for the different characters.

Dean grins. "For the record, you are my favorite life-form ever."

"Why do you talk about me like I'm a scene project?" I take another bite of the burger. No wonder people get addicted to fast food. Sure, I can feel the bleach or whatever they wash the meat in corroding my intestines, but it tastes like salt and fat, and how can that be bad?

Dean looks out the window. "Because if I talked about you the way I want to talk about you, you'd bolt."

I know I shouldn't ask him to explain, but I do anyway, trying to sound nonchalant. "How do you want to talk about me?"

He looks at me. No, he looks *through* me. His eyes are that intense. "Harley," he says, "I think I love you."

I don't know what to think or say. Every emotion in the book washes over me. I'm stunned. I'm elated. I'm pissed. I'm scared. And I want to cry. I go with the last one. I burst into tears at our table.

You know what they say. Third time's a charm.

～e๑

The ride to the next campground feels like sex. In spite of the wind, I'm profoundly conscious of Dean's breath on the back of my neck. I can tell the difference between regular air and

Dean air. Every molecule in my body is tuned into him. His legs wrapped around me might be the best thing that's ever happened to me. I feel alive. My blood pounds. My skin is electric. My eyes take in all the details. The sky is the kind of blue I saw that one time I smoked pot with Amy, a deep blue that doesn't exist in the regular world. The heat from the pavement burns me, and even though I don't believe in god, I think cheesy thoughts about divine breath rising from the ground. The voice-over in my head sounds like bad poetry. I keep hearing Dean say, "I think I love you," and all of this, the heat and the vivid blues and the poems in my head, makes me wonder if I love him back. Is this what love feels like? Hell if I know. Not like I've ever been in love before. All I know is whatever this is scares the crap out of me. Still, I can't back away from it. It's like a potentially deadly ocean I want to jump into, never mind the sharks.

When we finally pull over at a campground, Dean gets off, and then I do. I can barely stand, and it has nothing to do with being sore from riding the motorcycle. As I turn toward Dean, his eyes have that hungry look he had at the ocean. I want to jump into them and drown, just like that day. And now, I can't even blame it on the bourbon.

"Harley." Dean raises his hand toward my face and stops halfway, like he isn't sure I'll let him touch me.

"Dean," I whisper back, because I'm not sure what else I'm supposed to say. I want to make jokes, pretend I don't feel what I do, but all of the sassy has left me. I can't look at Dean and mock him. Not when looking at him makes me want to lick him. Did I just say that? Okay, it's out then. I want to lick

Dean like he is a Popsicle. The cherry kind. The best kind. The kind I would have beaten a neighbor kid to death for when I was six. Mom's cartoon sex book sure as hell didn't warn me about this intense emotion.

Dean finishes raising his hand. Tentatively, he runs his thumb over my cheek. This is the part of the story where I turn into a slutty sex fiend, like I did that day at the beach. Before Dean can do anything else, I lunge him and plant one on him. His lips taste so good. Better than a cherry Popsicle. Better than anything. I am the one who yanks a sleeping bag off the bike and unrolls it. I am the one who pushes Dean down and straddles him. I am the one who rips off his shirt, who unbuttons his jeans, who licks his belly like it is that Popsicle.

He doesn't ask me if it's okay this time. And later, when he's inside me, I look up at him. Loose curls frame his face. His skin is smooth, brown, shining. He watches me like I am an alien or a baby triceratops or a ticket to see John Lennon live, a strange, impossible, never-seen-before wonder. A miracle. The moon rises behind him, and because my mind is always stuck in a book, I think about the scene in *For Whom the Bell Tolls* where the earth moves. It's like that. The earth moves. And I don't have to wonder if I am in love with Dean anymore.

I know.

⁃❧

I wake up, and all of me hurts. I don't mean my body. Maybe that does ache. Maybe my back is sore. Maybe my neck is kinked. But it's what's happening inside me that makes me press my lips together. Only an act of sheer will keeps me from screaming. What have I done? Dean lies next to me, snoring softly. My head rests on his arm. He's naked. Above us, the sun is starting to rise, but it's already hot. Too hot. This is probably a gift because no one else is camping for fear of the heat. Smart people are huddled in their air-conditioned houses binging on Netflix. As far as I know, no unsuspecting hikers have stumbled onto our sex fest. But here we are, naked in the desert. A hawk watches from his perch atop a cactus a few feet away. His yellow eyes judge me.

I study Dean, the curve of his lips, the dent in his throat, the little tattoo next to his left nipple that says *unbroken*. I wonder what made him feel so defeated that he tattooed a permanent inspirational poster on his body. Inspirational posters tell you that everything is surmountable, that no matter what happens, you can come back from it, bigger and better than ever. But I'm not so sure about that. I wonder if someday Dean will regret that tattoo because it isn't true anymore. A person cannot remain unbroken forever.

Suddenly, I feel all the little cracks in me. A heart can shatter only so many times before it stops coming together again. I can tell you this for sure because I feel the fragility of mine. Mom's death has left me walking the dizzy edge of a precipice I don't dare contemplate. Sometimes, when I'm riding through LA, I see people on street corners mumbling to others who aren't there, and I think for a second that I'm inches away from understanding exactly what it's like to be them. I get how certainty disappears. I know how it is to scramble for solid ground and never find it. I look over at Dean. He smiles in his sleep like a kid, and I love him for it. Terror grips me. I know that if I keep loving Dean, eventually, he is going to break my heart. And then, it will explode like a vase dropped from a window.

Then I will never be okay again.

This is when I decide to end things with Dean. It's not a head decision. I'm not even sure I allow myself to think it straight out. But below my consciousness, the part of me that is like a rat trying to gnaw its way out of a cage knows it's going to do whatever it takes to get rid of him. Because deep down, all men are assholes. If my own father's absence didn't teach me that, my first sex partner did.

⁓℮⁓

So let's talk about the Asshole. No, this isn't an anatomy lesson. The Asshole is the name I gave the fucker who took my virginity. I was going to call him the Phony, but I don't want my sexual confession to sound like some female Holden Caulfield rip-off. So I settled for the Asshole. Neat. Clean. To the point.

I was still in the throes of recovering from the Asshole's betrayal when Mom met her untimely demise. The pain of that experience kinda got put on the back burner (no pun intended) after the fire. But it was still there, the broken limb that got overshadowed by a sucking chest wound. The agony generated by the potentially fatal injury took predominance, but that didn't mean the cracked bones didn't ache too from time to time.

I met the Asshole in fifth period geometry when he asked if he could copy my test answers. This should have been a red flag, but I'm notoriously bad at heeding warning signs. (*Do not leave candle burning while sleeping*, for instance.) Also, the Asshole had these crazy brown eyes and like twenty-four dimples. Okay, I may be exaggerating on the dimple count, but seriously, when he smiled, his face made this sweet, "Oh, my god, I'm so cute. Don't you want to do me?" expression. My answer to this silent question was a resounding yes. Not that I knew what doing someone felt like. I'd never done it. But after the Asshole smiled at me and asked if he could copy my test answers, I knew what it felt like to *want* to do someone. Did I mention that he ran his hand over the small of my back as he posed his questions, the verbal one about the Geometry, and the silent one about sex? 'Cause he did.

Not only did I let him copy my test answers, I also agreed to meet him to study at Lean Beans after school. Lean Beans was the coffee shop where all the cool kids hung out when they couldn't get their hands on illegal alcohol. They mainlined lattes and talked about bands mostly. I'd gone in there once, felt like a pariah, and never gone back. But if I went with the Asshole, I'd be accepted. It was a given. The Asshole was the hottest guy in the eleventh grade, if not in the entire school. He played in a band, Suck Pile Sauna, which got regular gigs in local bars, which meant he often *could* score illegal alcohol, which added to the already considerable adoration directed his way due to his dimples.

It turned out what the Asshole meant by "study" was "grope under the table," which for some reason was okay with me. Or I tried to be okay with it. At the time, I was very aware of the fact that I was definitively not popular and while I pretended not to care, I did. A lot. To have this god among acne-prone mortals interested in me made my head spin. I thought it was love. It looked like love looks in the movies, you know the bad ones from the eighties, like *The Breakfast Club,* where the hot guy falls for the weird girl, and they all live happily ever after in their castle on the football field? I thought it was going to be like that. I'd gone around for so long thinking I wasn't enough, I felt like a walking fraction. And since pretty much everything I'd ever seen, read, or listened to said the way to fix feeling like a half-of-something was to find your other half and fuck it, I was pretty much ready and willing to shove any boy who was interested into the empty space beside me. Or should I say inside me? I'd never expected someone like the Asshole to stumble into that role though. Not in a million years. And when he stuck his hand under the table and started to caress my thigh, I thought (this isn't an exact translation): *Holy crap! This kinda feels creepy, but so what, I'm going to be whole now!*

I'd like to say I made him wait a few weeks, or even a few days, but I didn't. I'd like to say I told him I was a virgin first, but I didn't do that either. What I did was invite him over for a "study date" the next day while Mom was off at her second job. I made a few pathetic attempts at resisting his concerted efforts to shove his hands up my shirt, after which he whispered, "But, baby, I love you."

My first response to his unexpected declaration was incredulity. How could he love me? He didn't know me. But my second response was elation. Of course he loved me! Wasn't I perfectly weird and lovable? Didn't that guy in *The Breakfast Club* love Ally Sheedy after only one day? So I decided to believe him. Fatal error, man. Didn't I learn anything from reading *Les Miserables* in that honors class I took? In that book, the cad tells poor, dumb Fantine that he loves her. He's lying (shocker), and she ends up pregnant and cast out of her home, begging for coal and bread. So I should have seen it coming. But I didn't, mostly because I didn't want to.

I wanted to be in a movie from the eighties, not a drama about the plight of fallen women. And I *definitely* didn't want to star in an educational short on how to avoid contracting the herp. Which is exactly what the Asshole and my short-lived love story turned out to be.

Long story short, I can thank the Asshole for teaching me that sex ain't all it's cracked up to be in the movies. It hurt, and it lasted less than a minute. He didn't even look at me while he did it. I was not one for all of that religious guilt, since I was decidedly agnostic, but still, as he rolled away from me, I couldn't help feeling dirty. Used. Which made me desperate. Which made me say, in this tinny, wussy-ass voice I'd never heard come out of my mouth before: "Call me in the morning." Also, as he was getting up, I may or may not have clutched at him in a not so subtle "Oh, for the love of Jesus, don't leave me" way. Which is sexy.

I don't even have to tell you that he didn't call me in the morning or ever again. I did, however, call him. Twenty-two times. I counted. While I was calling him obsessively, he was apparently wooing the leggy star of the track team who looked a hell of a lot like Angelina Jolie. Within a week of our "study date," my paramour was making out in the hallways with his new girlfriend. I spent months after that wondering what was wrong with me, comparing myself to every leggy, busty, lippy girl I saw. I seriously considered breast implants. And lip injections. I ran a Google search for "leg extensions" to see if it was a thing.

At first, I fantasized the Asshole would come crawling back to me. In my early fantasies, I forgave him. As time went by, I invented other scenarios. Him begging. Me scoffing. "What? You thought you were the only guy I was fucking? Get a grip." I imagined walking away after that, my head held high, my dignity restored. But I never got to say those words because the Asshole never so much as glanced my way again.

My attempts at restoring contact with my long lost love may have contributed to my new nickname around school: Psycho-Stalker Girl. So I guess sleeping with the Asshole did gain me notoriety, though not the brand I was after.

Truth be told, I was up for a new beginning after my run-in with the Asshole. Maybe the move to Los Angeles would have been well timed, had Mom come with me, but she didn't. And I'm not sure moving to a new school where you are completely invisible is necessarily a step in the right direction when you take the step with an urn full of dead Mom in tow.

In addition to the new nickname, the Asshole gave me the gift that kept on giving—chlamydia—which added a whole new level of "dirty" to an experience that had left me feeling like a walking toilet bowl. And that bit about him making me feel whole? Didn't happen.

Au contraire, mon ami.

He left me utterly shattered.

After the Asshole, I promised myself I'd never act like that about a guy again. I promised myself I'd be cool, aloof, and bulletproof. Anything but Psycho-Stalker Girl. And I was. You can ask Dean.

Religious people say we get punished for our sins, but I don't think that's always the case. I bet if you asked Dean, he'd tell you that sometimes, you get punished for other people's sins too.

FIVE

can picture my mom singing some song from the seventies about sex. She was two or three glasses of wine in, dancing around the kitchen in her nightgown, using our Chihuahua's paw for a microphone. The Chihuahua in question (Darwin, may he rest in peace) was extremely put out, being held and whirled. I must have been fourteen or fifteen when that happened, because before that, Mom never drank in front of me. Imagine my surprise when I hit my teens and discovered my mom was a closet lush. Not an AA-style lush. Once or twice a week, she'd have a few glasses of wine, let her hair down, two-step with the dog, and sing about sex. I have yet to follow in my mother's footsteps and bust out my best moves while singing about sex, but I think about it all the time. Not just about having it, but about what it means.

There are people who say sex is just another biological urge, no more emotionally significant than eating or drinking or peeing. They sleep with anyone they want, and they walk away, feeling nothing.

Then there are those who say sex is the most important thing a person can do. They think it has mysterious powers. They save themselves for marriage. They believe if they do it with the wrong person, they'll burn in hell forever.

I fall somewhere in the middle of these two camps. If there is a god, I can't imagine him or her or it being all worked up about people voluntarily bumping uglies when there are things like rape, war, and starvation in the world. I would think a god who prioritized policing people's consensual sex lives over saving babies from bombs might have a serious problem with his/her/its priorities. But I can't quite subscribe to the "sex means nothing" ideology either. I mean, how can you share the most secret parts of yourself with another person and not be changed in some way? Admittedly, under all of my leather and bravado, I'm kinda sappy, like Mom. I've felt eternally bonded to a person over the fact that we drank from the same cup. So sharing bodily fluids, the fluids that have the potential to make babies, feels like a big deal to me.

Speaking of which. My period hasn't started, in case you're wondering. I know what you're thinking. I should tell Dean, who sits behind me, holding my waist too tight as scenery rushes along beside us. There are several reasons I can't tell him.

1. The wind is loud.
2. If I try to have a serious conversation while I am driving a motorcycle, we will die in a fiery crash, and

there have been enough fiery deaths in my world for the time being.

3.   You want me to tell this guy I'm pregnant? Are you kidding me? You do understand that if I tell him, it's real, right? We are no longer two kids sharing a zany trip across the United States on a Harley (as zany as a trip transporting an urn full of parental ashes can be). We are now two young adults poised on the brink of disaster. We are now a cautionary tale. We are now an after-school special. I'm already an after-school special. My mom died in a fire I accidentally started, okay? So I really don't need the extra drama of an unplanned pregnancy. Yeah, I just said that. Unplanned pregnancy. I sound like a pamphlet you'd find in the waiting room at a doctor's office, right?

We pull over at a motel somewhere in the middle of nowhere. No matter how far we drive, everything feels like the middle of nowhere. In New York, if you walk ten feet without hitting a skyscraper or a Chinese deli or a theater, you have inadvertently wandered into a wasteland. But here, you can drive for miles and miles without seeing anything but cactus. So when I see this crappy, run-down motel called the TeePee Inn, complete with a cigar store Indian statue standing outside (apparently, they haven't quite outgrown that whole racism thing here in the Southwest), it looks like an oasis. I'm tired of sleeping on the ground. I'm tired of waking up wondering if the tickle on my foot is a scorpion or a blade of grass. And let's be real—if I'm going to get naked with Dean (which I probably am), I'd rather be in a place where we have less than a 42 percent chance of being discovered by hikers. So yeah, I spring for a motel. Most of the lights on the sign are out, so we aren't sure if VAC means "vacancy" or "no vacancy," but it turns out they have room. In fact, judging from the otherworldly (read "creepy") silence, I'm pretty sure we are the only customers.

"I bet this place is haunted," Dean says as I fumble with the key, which is an actual old-fashioned key, not a key card.

"I didn't even know they still made keys like this," I say, trying to change the subject because although I'm not sure I believe in god, I am 100 percent sure ghosts exist. Blame it on one too many episodes of *Ghost Hunters*.

"Seriously." Dean presses blithely onward, either unaware of my discomfort at his mention of ghosts or super aware and relishing it. It's hard to tell with him. "I think this place is haunted. I read something about it online."

"You're making this up," I say. Finally, the door to the hotel room springs open, revealing the ugliest bed known to humanity, a sagging dresser, and two very questionable paintings, both of which look like they have been damaged by rain. Or fire sprinklers. Or urine.

"I'm not making it up." Dean tosses his backpack on a hideous orange chair in the corner and heads to the bathroom. I can hear him peeing. Is it weird that I find the sound sexy?

"They said there was a massacre near here," Dean continues. "The army came in and killed a bunch of Navajo women in their sleep while the men were off hunting. The ghosts of the dead haunt this area."

I fall back on the bed. It smells like cigarettes and dirty bodies, which makes me think of an exposé about hotel rooms I watched once. If you shine a purple light on hotel beds, there are all kinds of gross things hiding in the sheets. I wonder if this comforter has ever been washed. "What do the ghosts do?" I call, deciding I'd rather think about ghosts than filth.

"Typical ghost stuff. Wailing. Turning lights on and off. You know the drill."

"Those ghosts need to up their game," I say, displaying more courage than I feel. "La Llorona drowns people." Overhead, the vent is covered with a thick layer of grime. I imagine ghosts slithering between the slats.

"La Llorona who?" Dean walks out zipping up his pants. I almost forget about ghosts. Almost.

"La Llorona is this Mexican ghost. She drowned her children to get revenge on her cheating husband, and then, she drowned herself. Now she wanders the land looking for kids to drown."

"Well, that's decidedly horrifying." Dean falls beside me. I totally forget about ghosts. "Hey, you." He touches my cheek. "Nice to see your face again."

"Not like we've been apart," I say.

"Yeah, but I spend most of my time looking at the back of your head. Which reminds me. Are you ever going to let me drive?"

"Nope." I touch his cheek too.

He kisses me. It tastes like mint, which means he brushed his teeth in the bathroom, which means he cares about impressing me, which is so damn sweet. I kiss him back, hard. We make out for a few minutes, and I can't believe how soft his mouth is and how much I love the hard line of his shoulders under my hands. Then the vent makes a clanking noise. I open my eyes. It has to be a ghost.

Apparently unaware our make-out session has been infiltrated by undead spirits, Dean presses blithely on, his eyes still closed. I'm afraid to close my eyes again, so I watch him, seeing mostly the little wrinkles in his forehead. And it occurs to me that I'm utterly in love with his hairline. This should probably make me get all romance-novel sweet, but it doesn't. Instead, a cold knot of dread forms in my belly, as if I'm about to step off a cliff. And I am desperate to pull myself back from the edge. I remember the way I felt in the campground and that unnamed urge to dump Dean and run. Looking up at Dean now, that seems like a really good idea. That rat inside me starts gnawing at its cage. "Set me free," it screams. Part of me hates that rat. Part of me knows Dean is the best thing that has happened to me in a long time. But another part of me, the part that is still an open wound after Mom's death, thinks the rat has a point.

Suddenly, Dean's lips don't taste sweet at all. My heart pounds in an impending panic attack. I pull away.

"Something wrong?" asks Dean.

I sit up, reaching for the remote control, and turn on the TV. I don't want to tell him what I feel. My pulse races.

Mentally, I run through all the heart attack symptoms I have read on the internet. My right arm *does* hurt a little. I'm short of breath.

It's only a panic attack.

"Um, okay, I guess we'll watch *Scooby-Doo,*" Dean says. "I wasn't enjoying kissing you anyway."

"That makes two of us," I snap. My head feels spinny. I think about Mom, how she was here one day, dead the next. It could happen to anyone.

Dean laughs. I fucking hate it when people think I'm joking when I'm not. That tearing sound overwhelms me. I hear Mom screaming. I hear Mercy saying, "Honey, your mom died." Shit. My heart races so fast; my chest hurts.

It's only a panic attack! I think again.

It doesn't help. I try counting physical objects. A bed. A dresser. A—shit, I'm dying. My lungs are collapsing. I can't breathe.

IT'S ONLY A PANIC ATTACK.

Inside my head, I scream the mantra. It sounds like an assault. I struggle to hold my body normally, staring at the screen as Scooby and friends unmask a balding villain.

Shit. Shit. Shit. I don't want Dean to know what's happening inside me. I don't want him to know how broken I really am. The thought of him knowing is scarier than the thought of dying. *I will not scream,* I think, which may sound crazy, unless you've ever had a panic attack. Then you know where I'm coming from. Again, I try to slow my breathing. I let my gaze dart around the room, looking for something, anything, safe to latch onto. Everything looks blurry. Scary. Even the clock is terrifying with its flashing red numbers, reminding me I only have so long to live, counting the minutes until my death. Shaggy laughs in that weird way that makes everyone over the age of nine believe he is a chronic pothead.

Someone knocks on the door. Dean sits bolt upright, his hair mussed. I yank my shirt down. I hadn't even realized my shirt was up until now.

"Yeah?" Dean calls.

"Pizza," says a muffled voice from the other side of the door.

"Did you order pizza?" Dean asks me.

I shake my head.

"We didn't order pizza," Dean says.

"It says you did. Room 118."

"Well, we didn't," Dean says.

My chest feels like a bomb went off in it. I don't care what that quack doctor said. I'm dying.

"Do you want it anyway?" asks the voice outside the door. "I don't know what else I'm going to do with it."

Dean looks at me, questioning.

Shrugging, I continue to will my breathing to slow.

Dean goes to the door. When he opens it, an Angelina Jolie look-alike stands there. Behind her, the desert sky stretches forever blue. It's horrifying, like an ocean full of invisible monsters.

"Hi!" Dean runs his hands through his hair. My boyfriend is hitting on some bitch, and I'm dying.

"Hi." She smiles. Her teeth are perfect.

They stand awkwardly for a few seconds. I have never seen Dean at a loss for words, but apparently, he is now. *In through the nose, out through the mouth.*

"So you still want the pizza?" she asks.

"Yeah!" Dean takes it from her. "Are you sure you don't mind giving it to us?"

"It's all yours," says the girl. "I'd eat it myself, but I've eaten so much pizza over the last year, I'd be more tempted by rat poison."

Dean laughs like she's Jim Carrey. "Let me get you a tip," he says. "I'd hate for you to come all this way for nothing."

It's getting harder and harder not to scream. Instead, I snarl, "We don't need to give her a fucking tip."

Dean looks at me like I've announced I'm from planet Vulcan.

"She's right," the girl says, seeming embarrassed. "I don't need a tip."

You. Are. Not. Dying, I tell myself.

"No, really," Dean says. "I'll get you a tip."

"I'm fine," the girl says. Before Dean can protest, she turns and walks away.

"Thanks for the pizza!" Dean calls after her apologetically.

The girl half waves in acknowledgment. She doesn't look back.

Dean closes the door. "Harley, what was that?"

"You tell me, Don Juan."

"What?"

"Do you think I didn't notice the way you were checking

her out?" I have that feeling again, the one where I'm watching myself spin out of control and can do nothing to stop it. Did Dean really check her out? My head isn't sure, but the hurricane in my belly says he did, and that's all that really matters to me in this moment. In other news, I'm dying. Did I mention that?

"I was so not checking her out," Dean says.

"Oh, give me a break."

"Harley, what the hell is going on?"

"What were you going to do?" My volume is rising. I should turn it down, but I can't. "Write your phone number on a ten-dollar bill and stick it in her waistband?"

"That's so unfair," Deans says. "This is nuts."

"So now you're saying I'm crazy?" I yell.

"I didn't say you're crazy," Dean says. "I said this situation is nuts. I didn't do anything wrong."

My entire body buzzes. Rage. Terror. It's hard to say what I feel. All I know is I have to get the hell out of here. I lurch to my feet and pick up my helmet. "I'm going for a ride!" I scream. "When I get back, I want you and your shit to be gone!"

"What's wrong with you?" Dean isn't yelling, but he's close.

"What's wrong with me? What's wrong with me is I don't want the father of my baby to be some…some whore-monger!" I shout. Did I mention I had this English teacher who was really into talking about the Bible as a work of literature? Apparently, I retained some of the archaic vocabulary he helpfully passed along. It's fun when biblical words come out to play during a fight.

Dean looks stunned. I think maybe he doesn't know what "whoremonger" means until he says, "Wait? The father of your baby?"

I gasp, realizing what I've done. There is no taking the information back. "My period is late," I snap, deciding to use the news as a weapon.

"I'm going to be a dad?" Dean asks.

For weeks after this moment, I will look back, trying to pause the action, trying to understand what I was thinking. Right here. Right now. In the moment that could change everything. In the moment that only retrospectively will reveal itself to be a crossroads.

Underneath the buzzing in my brain, I'm thinking about the Asshole, and also about all the shit I've learned about romance from books and television and songs. One of the lessons I've learned is that boys are the enemy. They aren't people. They don't have feelings. They don't cry. They just sit around and try to have sex with girls and then don't call the next day. Which is entirely unfair, because I was the one who didn't call Dean the day after we had sex. And clearly, he has feelings because he's standing in front of me, inarguably emotional. So the decent move would be to forget he's a guy and treat him like a person. Tell him I'm sorry for being a bitch and melt into his arms weeping about our maybe-baby. But I'm not ready to melt. I'm not a glacier. I'm a volcano on the verge of explosion.

Instead, I say, "Don't get your panties in a knot. I'm not even sure it's yours." He winces like I slapped him.

"What? You thought you were the only guy I was fucking? Get a grip."

As I walk out the door, I glance over my shoulder. Dean looks like he's trying not to cry. I should say I'm lying. I should say something. Anything.

I don't.

⁓ꙮ

So what you're probably wondering is how I came to murder my mother. Okay, maybe you're not. Maybe you're wondering why I treated Dean like shit when he clearly didn't deserve it, but I'll get around to that. Let's talk about the murder first.

Maybe "murder" is a harsh word. A lawyer Mercy knows told me murder implies intent, and I didn't mean to kill my mom, obviously. I loved her, which is a silly little phrase meant to express an emotion too profound to ever be conveyed in words. You know that forever feeling you get when you look at the ocean, the way you don't know what's going on here on planet Earth, but you're pretty sure that it's bigger than anything scientists or priests have yet postulated? That's my love for my mom. It made me feel mystery and knowing all at once. It made me understand whatever the shamans and scribes of yesteryear must have felt when they scribbled down their holy books. It was true religion.

After she died, I went to six therapy sessions. Then I decided counseling was a load of shit. Dr. Jellum, this fat guy with severe body odor, put the psycho in psychotherapy.

I tried to trust him, but even before I discovered he was a creeper, I found his comb-over unsettling. The swath of hair at the center of his bald spot always reminded me of that white, wispy stuff on corn on the cob, right under the husk. It was difficult to muster confidence in a partially peeled vegetable.

In the days before I caught him staring at my boobs while I sobbed on his couch, he asked me to recall the time in my life I felt the safest. I couldn't pick one moment because honestly, I always felt safe with Mom. I'd spent my entire existence in this cocoon of safety until she was gone, and I realized the world was a monster. It was like I'd been dreaming I was the star in a Disney cartoon when really I'd been bumbling around the set of *Saw*. Even the kittens were killers. Even the flowers had teeth.

So suffice it to say, my mother's death was absolutely an accident. No sane person deliberately kills off her safe place. Granted, I may not have done a stellar job of convincing you I'm sane, but believe me when I say that before Mom died, I was pretty a-okay, mentally speaking. I mean, sure puberty was a bitch. Losing-my-virginity bit the big one. But all of my crises were run-of-the-mill. No big mental disturbances. No panic attacks. No suicidal tendencies. No alcohol problem, give or take a few nights sneaking screw top wine with Amy. Just Mom and I, chumming it up, watching Mexican soap operas, making our way through our pretty average lives together, neither of us particularly exceptional to anyone except each other.

On the night that changed everything, I went about

my routine. Before bed, I walked to the pantry for a snack.
I perused my culinary options, noticing the house smelled
stale. I ate something. On my way back to the bedroom, I
saw the candle sitting on the hall table. I think it was vanilla
scented, though I could be wrong. Maybe Hawaiian Island?
There was this cool little hippie shop down the street from
our house in Brooklyn. Their homemade candles were the
shit, and Mom and I were determined to try every single scent
they had. Anyway, I lit it, and as the wick sputtered to life, I
thought maybe it was a bad idea. At least, I tell myself I did.
I don't really remember. It was one of many small, ordinary
actions I took that night. I brushed my teeth. I put on my
pajamas. I checked Instagram. (The Asshole's girlfriend had
posted another selfie in that low-cut top, pouting with her fish
lips. Of course she did.) I went to sleep.

Only later would I lend the action of lighting the candle
any more weight than the other routine actions I took that
night. Truth be told, it probably didn't occur to me that it
might be dangerous. Truth be told, I lit candles all the time.
The only difference between that candle and all the others
was that this one killed my mom.

As I was falling asleep, Mom came into my room. She
was wearing blue pajamas. I will always remember that. She
said, "How's my monkey?" Which is stupid. I was seventeen, and she still talked to me like I was seven at bedtime.
If she thought I would allow it, I bet she would have still
been reading me bedtime stories. But that's how Mom was.
She was the epitome of the word "maternal." I opened my

eyes, said "fine," and closed them again. Just like that, I shut out my last glimpse of her face. I didn't open my eyes again, not even when she stopped at the door and said, "I love you, kid."

That was the last time I heard her voice.

I didn't say, "I love you too." If I had, I could comfort myself with that. *The last thing I ever said to her was "I love you,"* I'd think as I was falling asleep at night. But it wasn't. I was too tired. I didn't answer her at all. The last full sentence I uttered, about a half hour before that, was, "Hey, Mom, where the hell are the Cheez-Its?" or something equally profound as I foraged in the pantry. I have pieced that much together. I was standing there, and I said something mildly snarky that conveyed my displeasure at how she had organized the kitchen.

Do ghosts float around thinking about the last things the living said to them? Do they wonder, "Why did she have to ask about Cheez-Its? Did my final moments have to be so inglorious?" I imagine that even for them, those last ten or so words they hear take on more resonance than all of the words they heard in their lives. Does my mom sit up on some ghost cloud wondering why the last words she heard before she shuffled off her mortal coil had to be about snack foods? Does she wonder why her daughter killed her? Does she think I'm an ungrateful bitch after all she did for me? I mean, she gave up everything for me, and I murdered her.

Intent or not, that's what it was.

I said the last time I heard Mom's voice is when she said, "I love you, kid." But I can't fool you, can I? You already know that wasn't the last time I heard her voice. The last time I heard my mom, she was screaming.

Here's the part I've never told you. When she died, she was screaming my name.

—ೞ—

As I turn onto the freeway, all the rage I've been feeling since Mom died gathers in my belly and rushes into my hand on the throttle. I hate Mom for dying. I hate god for letting her. I hate myself for killing her. I still feel like I'm dying, but I don't care anymore. I *want* to die. I squeeze hard, relishing the engine roaring in my ears and the pavement rushing along below me, getting off on the thought that one quick jerk of the handlebars is all that stands between me and certain death. It wouldn't be such a terrible way to die. There are worse ways to go out. Just ask my mom. Oh, wait, you can't. She's dead.

One day when I was little, Mom and I drove up on this accident. A biker had lost control of his motorcycle and ended up bleeding out on the asphalt. Either he or his bike had flown for a while. The motorcycle lay in a crumpled heap twenty feet away from the body. I wondered if it was the man or the motorcycle that soared up over the pavement. If it was the man, what did he feel as he was flying? Ecstasy? Terror?

Whatever he felt, it didn't last long because he was no longer with us. I just knew. He didn't look like a person anymore. Something vital was gone.

Well, yeah. His life was gone. Isn't that what *vital* means?

The accident was horrifying, all that blood, and yet, even then, I knew the horror was for us, the living. The dead man felt nothing. At least I thought he didn't. But maybe I was wrong. Maybe he was off floating on a cloud somewhere. Maybe he was standing by, invisible, staring in bewilderment at the hunk of bloody flesh that used to be his body. Maybe he was in hell.

Hell. Now there's a particularly sinister version of after-life entertainment. Whoever came up with that notion was a psychopath. I heard my mom burn for a split second. The sound of it was enough to torture me for the rest of my life. Any god who would burn someone over and over for all eternity is a god I'd rather not know. That's all I have to say. Lucky for me, I don't believe in god.

Still, speeding along, watching the trees whiz past, contemplating death, I pray anyway. "God, give me a sign." I don't know why I do it. You know how they say there are no atheists in foxholes? Maybe this—me barreling down the highway at seventy-two miles per hour with nothing but a steel horse standing between me and death—is my foxhole. And if it is, it's deep. I started digging it when I lit that candle. I dug some more when I fucked Dean on that beach. I hit the bottom when I told Dean the baby wasn't his.

Nothing happens. No lightning bolts. No epiphanies. No visions. Just me pretending I'm Mario Andretti, thinking death might not be such a bad idea. But then, another thought comes into my head. A baby may be growing in me. If I drive this motorcycle over the edge of a cliff, two lives might be lost. I know it's stupid. It's just an embryo. But when I think about it, I feel way less alone.

Warmth rushes through me, like that day on the beach with Dean. I think I might love the maybe-baby sleeping inside me. I start to cry again, and I slow down. Way down. A sign up ahead says EXIT HERE. I do. I don't know why. I guess it's because I asked for a sign from god, and I think it's possible god took me literally.

I turn into the town at the end of the exit, and it's small. Just a gas station, a convenience store, and some trailers, as far as I can tell. I pull up in front of the store and turn off my bike. A man in a cowboy hat walks by. "Nice ride," he says.

"Thanks." I yank off my helmet and wipe my face, hoping I don't look as shitty as I feel, and that if I do, the store isn't packed.

It's not. Inside, I'm the only customer. Rows of dusty food line the shelves. I don't think this place gets much business. I wander the aisles, picking up packets of beef jerky, bags of chips, and bottles of water. I eye these items nonchalantly and then put them back, knowing damn well I didn't come here for food. I meander until I find the aisle I'm looking for. Tampons. Diapers. Baby wipes. And pregnancy tests. I pick one up. "Quick response," it says. Do I want a quick response? Am I ready for that? Do I want to know at all?

I glance over at the counter guy. He's talking on his cell phone with his back to me. I imagine walking up to him and laying the test on the counter. It would be bad enough if it were a girl, but a guy? No way, man. I put the test back on the shelf and take a few steps toward the door. I stop, realizing that if I don't do this now, I may never do it. I may wait until I am as big as a house to admit I'm pregnant. And by then, my options for dealing with the pregnancy will be limited. If I'm pregnant, I'm pregnant. Pretending I'm not isn't going to make it go away, any more than pretending Mom isn't dead will make her come back. I walk back to the shelf, pick up the test, and glance at the guy. He's still on his phone.

My phone dings. I take it out. Dean has texted. Harley, we need to talk.

I slip my phone back into my pocket. Then I drop the test in too. The bell over the door chimes as I walk out.

SIX

Speed seems to be my demon today. I'm possessed by it. Now that I have the pregnancy test, I want to get it over with as quickly as possible. I should probably go back to the room, tell Dean the truth, and let him hold my hand while I take the test. But I can't. I'm not sure he'd believe the baby is his anyway. He almost certainly hates me. I can barely handle my own emotions. I don't need his piled on top of them. So instead of driving back to Dean, I race farther down the freeway—not as fast as before—until I come to the next exit. I pull off.

This town is similar to the last one—a few houses, a convenience store, a shabby motel. Which of these locations might be ideal for finding out whether or not I'm pregnant? I could break into one of the houses. I've already shoplifted. Might as well continue my career as a criminal. "Well, that escalated quickly," I imagine Dean saying, and I laugh in spite of myself. But I'm way too tired to bust out some unsuspecting homeowner's window. I settle for the motel. The proverbial two birds with one stone. I can take the test and then take a nap.

The girl at the counter is young, my age, maybe a year or two older. Her hair is black at the roots, blond at the ends. She drinks her Diet Coke and pointedly ignores me even though I'm two feet away and the only other person in the room.

"Hi," I finally say.

"Hi." She says it like a cuss word. She's clearly not happy to have a customer.

"Sorry to intrude," I say, matching her tone. "You have any rooms?"

She rolls her eyes as if I have an IQ lower than plankton. "Uh, yeah. You think we get many guests?" She waves her hand around, as if to say, "You see those fake flowers, that dirty watercooler, those lousy yellow couches? You really think people want to look at this shit?"

I am rarely daunted by rudeness. For some reason, this girl's rudeness gets to me. I feel myself tearing up, which makes me want to smack myself in the face with the buffalo sculpture on the counter. Before Mom died, I never cried in public. Never. What the hell is wrong with me?

The girl's face softens. "I'm sorry. It's been a shitty day."

"You're telling me," I say, swabbing at my face with the palms of my hands.

"Is it a guy?" she asks.

"Among other things."

She nods knowingly. "Me too. I just found out my

asshole boyfriend cheated on me. With my sister." She slurps her Diet Coke to punctuate her announcement.

"Wow," I offer, unnerved by her intimate confession. "That totally sucks."

"I know." She sets her soda on the counter angrily. "I swear, I'm gonna go all Lorena Bobbitt on his ass."

"Lorena Bobbitt?" The name rings a bell, but I can't remember who she is. "Is she a singer?"

The girl laughs. "No, she's that lady who cut off her husband's dick after he cheated on her. Threw it into the bushes." She mimes lobbing an imaginary penis into the lobby. I am officially disturbed. When I don't respond to her declaration of violent intentions, she presses on. "Is yours a cheater?"

"No," I say. "I mean, he checked out a pizza girl, but he didn't cheat with her."

"You seriously broke up with a guy for checking out a pizza girl?" she asks.

"I'm kidding," I say. For the first time, it occurs to me that I might be the asshole in this situation. I push the thought out of my head. Men are the assholes, not me. "It was more than that."

"Why'd you break up then?"

Did we break up? He's still back at the other hotel room waiting for me. "We weren't really officially together," I deflect. She looks at me and waits. Mercy's stupid waiting trick. Does everyone in the world know this? True to form, I spill everything. "I mean, we were having sex, and I might be pregnant, but we weren't together."

"Oh, sweetheart," she says. Did I mention that I hate it when people call me sweetheart? It makes me feel like I'm in an ancient episode of *Alice*.

"Yeah." I pull out the test and lay it on the counter. "I stopped here so I could take this."

She picks up the test, turns it over, and reads the back. "If it's positive, I'll totally take you out for a drink after my shift." She sets the test back on the counter.

I pause, stunned. "I'm too young to get into a bar, and besides, if it's positive, I'm pregnant." I pick up the test and tuck it into my pocket.

"I can totally get you a fake ID," she offers. She's clearly missing the point. "A friend of mine makes them on his computer. They're good. They look real. I mean, you can't use them in the bars that check them under those purple lights, but none of the bars around here have that shit."

"Yeah." I nod, wondering if I've crossed from an episode of *Alice* to an episode of *Jerry Springer*. "But even if I can get into a bar, I can't drink. I'm *pregnant*."

She blinks twice. I have time to observe her carefully painted eyelids. Blue sparkles. Her face finally registers comprehension. "Oh, shit!" She laughs. "If you drink, the baby will be a retard, right?"

Now I'm pissed. She called my maybe-baby a retard. "Something like that. Hey, can I get a room? I'm totally exhausted."

"Sorry!" She giggles like she thinks she's cute. She's not. On a scale of one to ten, ten being "cute," one being "I want to punch you in the goddamn face," she's a negative six. She forges on. "I'm such a space case."

I refrain from offering an opinion on her intellect.

As she rings me up, she talks about her cousin who just had a baby. "She's so screwed," she says, shaking her head. "Didn't even finish high school. Still lives with her mom. I feel bad for her. She never leaves the house, and she's all depressed and shit. I try to get her to go out, but she can never find a sitter."

I have a vision of myself sitting on Mercy's couch when I'm twenty, rocking a screaming toddler. Hey, at least I already finished high school. I've got that going for me.

"One or two keys?" she asks.

"One," I say.

"Oh, yeah! You're alone." She hands me a key. "Let me know if you change your mind about going out."

I fight the urge to leap over the counter and strangle her.

&

The pregnancy test is hard to open, which irritates me because shouldn't the makers know their customers will be dying of anticipation? Adding layers of impermeable cardboard and tinfoil to the already intolerable waiting game seems cruel. Obviously, though, the makers of pregnancy tests are sadistic monsters. It takes me a good minute to break into the packaging. It feels like a million years. Finally, I'm holding a thin stick in my hands. This seemingly insignificant bit of recyclable plastic holds my fate.

Remember when I said I thought I loved my maybe-baby? I'm not so sure anymore. Suddenly, I'm sick with fear. I tell myself that if there is no maybe-baby inside me, I will go out and celebrate with Glitter Eyelids from the front desk. Why not? I'll be up for a drink. Hell, I'll be up for ten.

I read the instructions. All I have to do is pee on the stick, and then, the test will give me a pink plus sign if I'm a pregnant, a blue negative sign if I'm not. I sit on the toilet and hold the stick in a stream of my urine. I piss on my hand, of course, because it seems to be that kind of day. Week. Month. Year. Life.

Shaking, I set the test on the counter, wash my hands, and look in the mirror. My mom was as nontraditional as moms get, but I still can't wrap my head around the scrawny-ass biker chick in the mirror being a mother. I think about the prospect of trading my motorcycle for a Honda with a car seat in back. My head starts to spin. I lift my long hair and curl it under so it resembles a short bob, trying to picture myself with a soccer mom haircut. I can't. I glance over at the test. My stomach clenches. It's already changing.

Pink.

My eyes burn. I pick up the stick and stare at it. "No, no, no! Blue, blue, blue!" It doesn't listen. The plus sign gets pinker.

I drop the stick in the sink and lean my head against the cool mirror. As I pull away, I look at myself again. It's official. Soccer mom cut or no, I'm pregnant.

My phone dings. Dean again. I need to know what's going on.

I stare at the screen. Why can't he leave me alone for two minutes?

Fuck. Off. I type.

I press Send. Then I wander out of the bathroom and fall onto the queen-size bed, still clutching the pregnancy test. The bed is softer than the one I shared with Dean. It doesn't smell like cigarettes. There are no ghosts.

When I was a little girl, I had this trick. When things got hard, I'd sleep so I wouldn't have to feel anything. If I got an F on a test, I'd sleep. If my dog died, I'd sleep. If the kids at school made fun of me, I'd sleep. Sleep was my drug, my saving grace. Since Mom died, I haven't been able to do that. Sleep eludes me. But now, my old trick comes back to me like I never forgot how to do it in the first place. I close my eyes, force myself not to think, and before I know it, I'm lost in sweet, black nothing.

SEVEN

When I wake up, it's dark. I don't know where I am. Then everything comes rushing back. The fight with Dean. The positive pregnancy test. I fumble for the light switch and flip it on. The test sits next to me on the bed. I pick it up. The pink plus sign is still there mocking me.

The clock says 11:14. Panicking, I jump up. How the hell did I sleep for that long? Sleep has melted my rage and now all I feel is horror and regret. I have to get back to Dean and fix this. I pull out my phone. The last text I sent stares at me from its little green bubble.

Fuck. Off.

Oh, god. Shoving the test into my pocket, I grab my backpack and head for the door. As I walk through the lobby, Glitter Eyelids looks up. "Oh, shit," she says. "Positive?"

I guess I'm doing a stellar job of playing it cool. "Don't you ever go home?" I ask.

She smiles, seemingly unaware that my question wasn't well intentioned. Apparently, her sarcasm meter is broken. "I'm working a double."

Like I give a crap. I shove the door open.

"If you want to go for a drink, I'm off at midnight," she calls after me.

"I'm good!" I step out into the muggy heat.

As I walk through the parking lot, the night is alive with noise. Crickets, cars, and somewhere far away, a storm. I hate it when the world echoes my mood, as if it's creating a sound track for my bullshit life. Like I need thunder rolling in the distance to enhance the dread in my gut.

I start my bike and pull back onto the freeway. A voice inside me tells me to text Dean and let him know I'm okay. The voice sounds a lot like Mom. *Say you're sorry, and tell him he's the only one,* I can almost hear her whisper. If it is Mom, I don't know what she's thinking. I was never very good at talking about my feelings. I don't think I ever apologized to her once, even when we argued and I called her a bitch.

She and I had been fighting about cleaning the bathroom. She'd been asking me to do it for days, and I'd been pointedly ignoring her. Finally, she lost it. "Do I have to do everything around here?" she asked, tossing my toothbrush into the drawer. "I'm not your maid!"

I knew she had a point but didn't want to admit it. Instead, I went to my room and slammed the door. When she knocked a few minutes later, it pissed me off that she couldn't leave me alone to cool down. "Go away, you bitch!"

I was fourteen at the time, going through puberty. I know my hormones were out of control, but I still feel guilty every time I think about that day. If I could change one thing in my whole life (besides the fire, obviously), it would be that.

I didn't say I was sorry though. Instead, I climbed out my window, took a train to the beach, and collected a basket of seashells, the ones Mom loved, the ones that looked white and ugly on the outside but inside were radiant, pearlescent blue. When I returned hours later, she was sitting on the couch, looking like she'd been crying. She swiped at her cheeks.

"I got these for you," I said.

"Thank you, kid." She came to me and kissed me on the head. "God, baby. I was worried sick about you. I was about to call the cops. Next time you're leaving, tell me, okay?"

I nodded. We never talked about the incident again.

I decide to do something similar for Dean. I pull over at a twenty-four-hour convenience store. It's lit up from the inside, bleeding neon light into the sweaty night. I walk in, and a scrawny, old guy slouches behind the counter. He has this weird mustache. It looks like an aging hamster attached itself to his top lip.

"Hi, sexy," he says.

Oh, dear god. What a perv. Ignoring him, I head for the back of the store.

He doesn't get the hint. "You fill out those jeans NA-ICE!"

I am impressed at his ability to turn one-syllable words into two.

"Dude," I say, "even if I was into creepy old men, that

pedo-stache would be a deal killer. Now leave me alone, or I'll come in here tomorrow and file a complaint. Bet your boss would love to hear how you treat customers."

He seems to think about saying something not very na-ice, then thinks better of it.

I go to a rack filled with key chains. One that says *Harley-Davidson* jumps out at me. I grab it, deciding that I will give Dean the key to my bike. He's always wanted to drive it.

I don't want to talk to the creep at the register, so I throw a ten on the counter and keep walking. He says something as I'm leaving, but I can't hear it over the jingling of the doorbell. I roll.

When I get back to the hotel, our room is dark. I knock on the door. No answer. I knock again. "Dean, it's me." Nothing.

On cue, thunder rolls. Fighting back panic, I walk around the hotel to the lobby. The door is locked, but a sign says RING BELL FOR NIGHT ATTENDANT. I ring it. Once. Twice. Three times.

Finally, a short, bleary-eyed woman comes out. "What do you want?" she demands. Clearly, this establishment does not pride itself on exceptional customer service. Normally, I'd say something snarky. But I'm too scared to care.

"I seem to have locked myself out of my room," I say.

She rolls her eyes. "Which room?"

"Room 222."

"Your boyfriend checked out an hour ago," she snaps.

I stare, stunned. "Are you sure?" I finally ask.

"He woke me up," she says. "Made me call him a cab."

"There are cabs out here?" I ask.

She snorts as if I'm an idiot. "The train station is twenty minutes away. Of course there are cabs."

"Oh."

"I assume you want back in?" she asks.

I feel like barfing. Not knowing what else to do, I nod. She rustles around behind the desk and slaps the key on the counter.

"Thank you," I mutter.

Clutching the key, I wander back to the room and unlock the door. When I turn on the light, the ghost of Dean stands there, crying because of the horrible things I said.

The pizza box still sits on the bed.

"Fuck you!" I say, meaning it, but not to Dean. Who am I talking to? Mom? God? The stupid pizza girl? I rush to the bed and throw the pizza as hard as I can. It hits the floor with a disappointing thud. What I want is a crash. What I want is broken glass.

As I set my backpack on a chair, I notice a piece of paper on the nightstand. I pick it up and read:

Harley,

Do you know why you're the only girl I've been with? Maybe this makes me a pussy, but I was waiting for someone special. I had chances with other girls, but they all felt wrong. And then I met you. I never told you this, but I loved you the first time I saw you sitting under that dock. I know it's pathetic, but I did. I sat here all day waiting for you, trying to tell myself I didn't love you anymore. The truth is, I still do. I always will. But I love me too. And if you've been lying to me, seeing other guys, I'm an asshole for sticking around. We need to figure out this baby thing. If it's mine, I'll do whatever I need to do.

Dean

I wad up the note, fall on the bed, and curl into a tiny ball. The fetal position. The baby inside me is sleeping just like this.

Dean was right about ghosts. They are everywhere. Maybe not everywhere. Maybe only inside my head. They scream like Mom. They cry like Dean. They have eyes like black holes that go on and on into forever, sucking me back into the past. The ghosts talk about how important seconds can be, how they can make or break you. Again and again, they show me that night I lit the candle. I see the flame leaping from the lighter, the wick sputtering to life. How long did that take? Two seconds? Three? An act that burned my world to the ground. And today with Dean, I did it again. Turns out I am good at incinerating the things I love. I'm a regular pyromaniac.

I think about going after Dean. How far can he have gotten? I consider texting him. I'm sorry. Come back. I type the words and then delete them. I'm not ready to talk to him.

I'm not ready to hear him say all the horrible things he must want to say to me right now.

Instead, I lie on this stinky motel bed, holding my belly, wondering if the gnawing there has something to do with the pregnancy or if it is simply the empty spot Dean left when he walked away. I hear Dean saying, "I love me too." And I want him to be standing in front of me so I can say, "You aren't the only one in this room who loves you. *I* love you, Dean." I type out those words, then delete them too.

My last text to Dean glares at me.

Fuck. Off.

"I'm such a bitch," I whisper.

I think about Dean's Navajo ghosts. I never thought I'd feel this way about poltergeists, but the notion is hopeful. If American Indian women can hang around for centuries after their deaths, maybe Mom could be hanging around too. "Momma," I say. My voice breaks between the m's in the middle; it shatters like glass.

I hear Mercy say, "Honey, your mom died." I mean I really *hear* it. More than I heard it in the hospital that day. More than I've heard it in the ten thousand times I've remembered it since then. It's real. Mom's dead. I remember when the coroner first handed me that jar of ashes. *This is all that's left of her*, I thought. I stared at the jar, waiting for her to scream again from inside, the way she did during the fire. She didn't.

I look around the empty motel room. A noise comes out of my mouth, more than a cry, more than a scream, more than a wail. It's a noise I never knew I could make. It's grief incarnated as sound.

"Momma," I whimper again.

Mom's ghost doesn't answer. I am utterly, irreversibly alone.

EIGHT

Every day, I wake up with a song in my head. I don't know why. Maybe it's because music is the only friend I have so I'm bound to hear its voice in my dreams. I believe that the song I wake up with is an omen for the next twenty-four hours, mostly because the day I set the house on fire, I woke up with Pink's "Funhouse" in my head. I should have known waking up hearing a song about burning a house down was bad news.

My omen theory isn't always accurate. For instance, last year when I found out I had gotten chlamydia from the Asshole, I woke up with Three Dog Night's "Joy to the World" in my head. No shit.

A song about dancing fishies was my omen for mother-fucking chlamydia, which turned out not to be that big of a deal, medically speaking, though there was a fishy smell involved. (Maybe it *was* an omen after all.) I only had to take a round of antibiotics to get rid of it.

Emotionally speaking, I was a train wreck. I had to sit on a cold table in a hospital gown under the gaze of Mom's very disapproving ob-gyn, who gave me a lecture about condoms and told me I was lucky I hadn't contracted HIV or gotten pregnant. As if I wasn't already traumatized by losing my virginity to a douchebag who said he loved me before he fucked me and never called again, the doctor offered to show me how to put a condom on a banana.

"No, thanks," I told her. "I took sex ed."

Apparently, I was a bad student. The first time I had sex, I didn't use protection and got an STD. The second time I had sex, I didn't use protection, and I got pregnant. Am I the stupidest/unluckiest person in the world or what?

Today, my omen theory is proven right. I wake up with that old Tori Amos song "A Sorta Fairytale" in my head. What blows my mind about music is that it's capable of replicating feelings exactly. I could tell you my heart was broken, and it might not mean shit to you. I could paint a broken heart, and you might think of Valentine's Day. But if I played "A Sorta Fairytale" for you? Well, it sounds exactly like a broken heart. It sounds like emptiness and longing and the death of dreams.

Because of that damn song, I remember Dean is gone before I even open my eyes, which seems unfair. Shouldn't I have a few moments of peace before reality comes rushing in? I bury my face in the stinky hotel pillow and "cry it out," as Mom would call it. Whenever I scraped my knee or got picked on, she'd hold me and say, "That's it, kid. Cry it out."

When my sobs subside, I get up and go to the bathroom. I almost laugh at how ugly I look. My eyes are swollen halfway shut. My skin is mottled. I'm pretty sure my hair has snot in it. I can't quite laugh though because there is a chasm in my belly—you know, the kind of emptiness that grows in you when the worst thing that could possibly happen has happened. I'm pretty fucking familiar with this particular brand of pain. Angrily, I slough off my clothes and turn on the shower. I step in.

"Shit!" It's cold. I back out of the water, turn the knob, and step back in. "Shit!" It's hot. By the time I finally get the temperature adjusted to an acceptable level, I'm sure I have both frostbite and third-degree burns. I wash my hair with a crappy motel shampoo and pat myself dry with a suspiciously unwhite towel. I'm afraid to really commit to the drying process because I'm almost 100 percent certain the towel smells like someone else's ass, which means it hasn't been washed in god knows how long.

When I'm done combing my hair, I throw on a pair of jeans and a T-shirt, grab my bag, and head for the door. I glance around to make sure I'm not leaving anything behind. The pitiful pizza is wadded up against the wall, looking desperate and alone. "You and me have a lot in common," I say to it. It occurs to me that I've finally completely lost my mind. I'm talking to Italian food. I see an image of Dean walking out, and my eyes burn. Instead of crying, I get pissed. "Fuck you," I tell the pizza, wondering what this particular cuisine did to deserve so much abuse. It had the nerve to be toted by a supermodel. That's what it did. Why couldn't the delivery girl have been the female equivalent of the dad on *Family Guy*? Why couldn't she have acne and an odor problem? Then Dean would still be here. We would be curled up together in that ugly bed, probably having just had sex. He would smell like deodorant and sweat and sunshine, which actually does have a smell. Any biker knows this.

"Hasta la vista, baby," I say to the pizza. It doesn't answer. I turn and walk out the door.

My motorcycle doesn't want to start, which is just like her. She rarely starts easily in the mornings. Usually, I coax her, muttering encouragement. Today, I kick her. She responds and sputters to life.

The seat burns me through my jeans. I'm grateful for the pain. I need something to snap me back into reality. I wonder if there is a hidden camera somewhere. I have to be the brunt of some cosmic joke, right? No way this can be real. I mean, it was bad enough with Mom's death, but now this? I imagine celebrities jumping out from behind the bushes yelling, "You got punk'd!"

"I got punk'd!" I scream as I start the bike. I must look like a crazy person, but I don't care. I pull out onto the road, then out onto the freeway again. I drive until I see golden arches beckoning. As I pull into the McDonald's parking lot, the weight of my predicament descends on me. It's like someone turned the sky into a slab of concrete and dropped it on my head. Holy shit.

I take off my helmet and stare at the horizon. Wavy lines of heat rise from the pavement. Birds flurry above a lone tree. Cars roar by on the freeway. I rub my eyes, trying to clear my vision, hardly believing there is a potential human growing inside of me, and I have to figure out what to do with it. Hell, I can barely decide what to eat for lunch most days.

For the first time, I think the word *abortion*. A surge of relief comes with it. I could walk into a clinic, and this whole thing would be over. Dean would come with me. I know he would. Even if he hates me now, he wouldn't make me go through that alone. But the thought of putting an end to my maybe-baby makes me sick to my stomach. I remember that feeling I had on the highway, like I loved the possibility of it. I remember the way thinking I loved that maybe-baby stopped me from crashing into a tree.

It's not that I think abortion is bad. Mom was pro-choice. She told me she never had doubts about keeping me, but she wanted women to have the option of choosing abortion if that was the best decision for them. She believed so strongly in abortion rights that she went to a lot of pro-choice rallies. Sometimes, I went with her. And I still believe in all that. I don't want women to have to get back alley abortions. I don't want women not to have the right to choose what to do with their own bodies. But somehow, now that it's my decision, the thought of abortion seems scarier than it ever did when it was an abstract idea. Now, it's a fetus. A real, live fetus. And if I let it grow, it will become a baby. And if it becomes a baby?

Well, if it becomes a baby, I'm screwed.

"Mom," I whisper. "How was this so easy for you? How did you know what to do?"

I look over and see a small kid staring at me from a car in the drive-through. He's cute—red hair and a curious expression. I wave at him, and he waves back, smiling tentatively. When he doesn't look away, I start to feel awkward, so I head inside.

Waiting in line, I remember Dean feeding me my very first McDonald's cheeseburger. How stupid is it that the two things that remind me irrevocably of my boyfriend, or whatever the hell he was, are cheeseburgers and bourbon? This has to be a bad sign, right? How could a guy like that be good for me? For a second, I think about what it might be like if Dean and I decided to raise this baby together. I imagine us living in some apartment in LA, working odd jobs, taking turns babysitting, trying to make ends meet. I bet Dean would be a great dad. I bet he'd be one of those guys who throws the kid up in the air and catches her or him making weird "*bub bub bub*" noises and laughing.

"May I take your order?" The woman behind the counter is forty-five. Maybe fifty. I wonder what life events lead her to work at McDonald's at her age. Normally, I probably wouldn't think anything of it, but right now, everything is about babies. So fair or not, I can't help but think she probably had a kid when she was nineteen. My fantasy about Dean and the "*bub bub bub*" noises evaporates.

"I'll get the two cheeseburgers meal," I say, because if

there is one thing in the world that is better than one cheese-burger, it has to be two.

"That'll be six dollars and seventy-eight cents." The woman manages as a smile as I hand her a ten, but she looks tired. I wonder what she will do when she goes home tonight. Sit on a cheap couch and watch Netflix? Drink whiskey?

When my food comes, I take it to a table near the ball pit and watch kids scramble around. There's this one girl wearing overalls with zebras on them. She has these amazing spiral curls, and she never stops squealing with delight. Normally, the noise might bother me, but as I shove the cheeseburgers down, I try to imagine that she's mine. A wave of love washes over me. I take in her rounded nose, her wide eyes, and her tiny fingers. I get why mothers love their kids so much. I think of my own mom, the way she loved me. It didn't matter what I did wrong, how badly I screwed up, she was always on my side. I touch Mom's sun necklace, and tears spring into my eyes. I give myself an internal lecture. *No more nervous break-downs while eating cheeseburgers.*

Miraculously, it works. My eyes dry up. Carefully, I unclasp the necklace and look at the silver orb resting in my palm. I turn it over to read the words engraved on it. *Los Milagros.*

"No matter what anyone said, I always knew you were my miracle." How was Mom so sure? Because the truth is, I'm not. I don't know if the fetus growing in me is a miracle or the worst thing that ever happened to me.

My cheeseburgers are gone. I wolf down the fries, toss my trash, and head outside.

"Awesome Harley," a woman says as I climb on.

"Thanks," I say.

"You live around here?" she asks.

"Nah. Just passing through."

"Where you headed?" she asks.

I'm about to say New York when it occurs to me that's not where I'm going anymore. Mom was sure she wanted to keep me in Omaha. Maybe I'll be sure about my decision in Omaha too. In my memory, I hear Mom's lecture about the highway of diamonds. "You take the next step in front of you, the one that shines." I'm not sure if Omaha shines, exactly, but it feels more right than New York. And I'm not exactly in a hurry to end this road trip anyway. There is nothing waiting for me in LA except Mercy, some flies, and an ex-best friend/baby daddy who now hates me.

"Omaha or bust," I say, and I start my bike.

‒℮

The winds do not come sweeping down the plains in Oklahoma. I don't care what the song says. What happens is the air hangs thick and damp, engulfing your already overheated body like a wet blanket. It smothers you, even when you are on a motorcycle, and the air should be rushing and free and wild. Nothing in Oklahoma is rushing and free and wild. I thought I hated Texas, but I hate Oklahoma more. Little clouds of bugs loom everywhere, ready to make a snack of your flesh if you stop to pee. The scenery is green, but it's the kind of endless, menacing green that seems to conceal secrets. Snakes. Biting insects. Dead bodies. Every few miles, some billboard tells me about Jesus or abortion. In Oklahoma, these two things seem to go hand in hand. I'm not a Jesus freak, but I do know a thing or two about the guy, thanks to that Bible-obsessed English teacher. I can tell you definitively that Jesus was a pretty hip dude. I could totally be down with him if I felt like the religion that bears his name had even one thing to do with his teachings. He was big on loving your enemies, feeding the poor, and not judging. He never once mentioned abortion. I'm pretty sure it wasn't even a thing in his day.

But the Oklahoma version of Jesus is all about abortion. One sign reminds me that Jesus died for my sins. The next reminds me that abortion stops a beating heart. As if I didn't already know that. As if I didn't already understand that weight of the decision hanging over my head. I wonder what would happen to this baby inside me if I decided to keep it. What kind of life could I give it? Would it go around hungry, lonely, wearing hand-me-down jeans to day care while its mom slaved away at some fast-food restaurant? Would it cry on Christmas because its friends got Xboxes, and all it got was a lousy T-shirt? My mom did a great job raising me alone, but like I've said, it wasn't easy. Also, she was twenty-two. Not eighteen. I'm not old enough to legally drink, but I still have to figure out what to do with a baby. It doesn't make sense. Nothing makes sense. Mom used to tell me that life wasn't fair, but I had no idea how true that was.

I pass a campground and wish that Dean was still on the motorcycle behind me. What would he have said if I told him I was pregnant in a less catastrophic way? Something right. Something beautiful. Something perfect. Then we would have curled up in a sleeping bag under the stars. He would have rested his thick fingers on my belly and whispered to me. I try to imagine his words. What would they be? I can't for the life of me conjure the sentence that would make all of this less apocalyptic.

I realize I'm crying again. I notice bits of trash nestled in the grass beside the road. The whole world seems tainted. Dirty. I want to barf. Which may be morning sickness in the afternoon. Or it may be the fact that I'm about to have a panic attack. I pull over at a rest stop, walk to a bench, and yank out my phone. Breathing deeply, trying to calm my roiling stomach, I scroll through the numbers. When I come to the M's, I stop on *Mom* and stare at the word, along with the little octopus emoji beside it.

Mom always ended her texts to me with random emojis. She thought they were so cute—the tiny monkeys, elephants, and cows. She'd write *I love you, kid* and punctuate it with a fried shrimp. She declared once that life was immeasurably better for humans in the 21st century because we had the capacity to punctuate our sentences with eggplants. So the octopus by her name in my phone was a tribute to her weird-ness, her sweetness, her innocence, her capacity to believe that all it took to make the world a better place was a pixelated cartoon squash.

I hit Mom's number and listen to it ring. In the weeks after her death, I did this fifty times a day, so I could hear her voice say, "Hi, this is Mary. Leave me a message, and I'll call you back. Have a kick-ass day!" I haven't called the number in months though, mostly because the sound of Mom's voice started making me feel like my brain was spinning out of control, like I might fall off the edge of sanity and never come back. This time, Mom's voice doesn't come on the other end. Instead, I get a prerecorded message. "The customer you are calling is unavailable. Please try again later."

I end the call. Mom's message is gone. It's more than I can handle. I can try again later, but it won't change the result. Mom's voice is never coming back.

Burying my face in my hands, I stifle the scream rising in my throat. Mom's voice may be gone, but my own voice is begging to be heard, and if I don't let it out, I'm going to lose it. I have to talk to someone. Anyone. Who? Dean? No way. I'm not ready for the level of groveling that would be required for a conversation with him. And even if I did grovel, who says he would forgive me and let me speak long enough to reveal that the baby really is his? More than likely, he'd tell me to fuck off as soon as I said hello. More trauma is exactly the thing I do not need.

I scroll through my contacts again. The list is short, so it doesn't take long. *Mercy.* I tap her name, and the phone starts to ring. I've been texting her every night, but it's all been quick, easy stuff. Lies, actually. Today was great! and I'm having the time of my life!

Just when I think Mercy isn't going to answer, she does. "Hey, kid." Her voice is happy. "What's up? How's the trip going?"

I consider continuing the charade by faking my way through a normal conversation about motels, campgrounds, and bad road trip food, but I can't lie anymore. "Mercy," I whisper. Even to me, my voice sounds shattered.

"What is it? Harley, what's going on? Are you okay?"

"No," I whisper. "Not even a little bit."

And I spill it. Everything. Dean leaving. The pregnancy. The fact that I came very freaking close to driving my motorcycle off the road on purpose. When I'm done, Mercy's quiet. If she's using her waiting trick, it's really not going to work this time, because I have nothing left to say.

"Harley, you need to come back to LA," she finally says. "We'll get you to a doctor." She doesn't reprimand me for the unprotected sex, for my cruelty to Dean, for my almost-suicide attempt. The only thing she seems to care about is me being okay. Like Mom would have.

"Come home, kid," Mercy begs. And for the first time since Mom died, I feel like I might still have a place to call my own in this world. Still, I can't go there. Not now. Not until I figure my shit out.

"Mercy, I love you, but I can't do that. Not yet." I know I have to finish what I started. I have to get Mom's ashes back to New York.

"Why not?" Mercy asks. "I'm worried about you." Her voice breaks. "I can't lose you too."

Suddenly, it hits me how much Mom's death has affected Mercy. She's been trying to stay steady for me, but underneath the facade, she's crushed, like I am. If I had driven my motorcycle off the road, she probably never would have been happy again. It occurs to me that my life, my choices, affect more than just me. "I won't die," I say. "I promise." I mean it.

"You almost killed yourself."

"I did, but I won't again." I remember Mom dancing around the kitchen with her glass of wine, pretending to be happy, and I wonder suddenly how much pain she was dragging around. How often did she make herself strong for me? If she could do it, I can do it. I'm going to make the right choice for me, for this baby in my belly, for Mercy, for Mom, for everyone. I'm going to be bigger than just me. "I'm going to figure this shit out," I say. "I'm going to get back on track."

"Maybe you should call Dean," Mercy suggests. "You could explain what happened, how scared and upset you were when you said the baby wasn't his."

I think she's right, but I can't. Not right now.

"I'm not ready for that," I say.

"All right, kid." Mercy still sounds worried. "Will you at least see a doctor? I can find a Planned Parenthood for you."

And she does. It's in Kansas City, which I will have to drive through to get to Omaha. I'm glad it's not in Oklahoma. I hope there won't be protestors standing outside the clinic, waiting to call me a murderer and press pictures of dead fetuses into my hands. I'm 100 percent sure that if there are, I will fall apart right there on the sidewalk. Just explode like a human time bomb and seep into the cracks in the cement.

If I had to handle one more bit of cruelty, I'm pretty sure I would die.

NINE

In Kansas City, there are no protestors. In fact, the clinic is utterly unremarkable. It's small and painted pale green, seemingly deserted but for a few cars parked outside. Still, I'm nervous as I dismount. What will happen to me in there? Will they pressure me to have an abortion, as the pro-lifers at the protests Mom and I attended shouted they would? Will there be menacing machines and sharp objects? Will I leave feeling disgraced, burdened, and broken forever?

I step into the lobby, and a gush of air greets me, cooling my overheated body. I'm grateful.

"Hello," a pretty woman says from behind the counter. "May I help you?"

Here goes. "Uh, yeah, sure," I say. "I have an appointment."

She looks down at the calendar on her desk. "Juliet Young?" she asks.

"Yeah," I say. "But you can call me Harley."

"Harley it is." She presses a clipboard full of papers into my hand. "Just fill these out, and Dr. Scapple will see you soon."

Dr. Scapple. Shit. Once, I heard of a dentist named Dr. Hurt. *Why didn't he change his name?* I thought. Dr. Scapple for a gynecologist is almost as bad. Immediately, my overactive imagination is barraged with a litany of scary metal instruments.

"Scalpel, like the knife used in surgeries?" I ask.

She laughs. "No, S-C-A-P-P-L-E, like an apple with 'sc' at the beginning."

"Still," I say. "He might want to think about changing his name."

"Dr. Scapple is a she." The woman smiles. "And I'll pass along your recommendation."

Shit. Why did I automatically think my doctor was a man? How unfeminist of me. Mom would be so disappointed.

I sit down in an overstuffed brown chair and fill out the paperwork.

Name. Date. Medical history.

What brings you in today?

That question makes me dizzy. I pause, then write *pregnant*. And voilà, it's a new level of real. I'm a pregnant girl sitting in a Planned Parenthood waiting room. Jesus H. Christ on a pogo stick, I'm a walking after-school special.

After I turn in the paperwork, a nurse comes out and invites me to follow her. I watch her gray ponytail bounce as she leads me to a scale.

"Let's get your weight," she says, smiling.

Nervously, I step on. Some girls are terrified of gaining

weight. My fears run the other direction. I'm as skinny as a noodle. I can never gain weight, even when I try. People always say I'm lucky, but I don't feel lucky. Just scrawny and ugly. I wish I could be curvy and beautiful like Amy, who looked like Jessica Rabbit might look if she were actually human. I guess if I want to be a silver-lining kind of girl, I can feel good about this pregnancy because it will undoubtedly make me gain weight.

"One hundred eighteen pounds," says the nurse. "You're a little underweight." She probably thinks I'm anorexic. Most people do.

"I know," I say defensively. "And no, I don't have an eating disorder." Maybe it's overkill, but I want to stop the "you know, we have some good counselors" lecture before it starts.

"I didn't say you did." She smiles reassuringly and leads me to an exam room, where she hands me a dressing gown and a plastic cup. "Please put this on. And we will need a urine sample. Just leave it on the back of the toilet."

"Kay," I say, feeling awkward. I remind myself she does this every day. I can't imagine having a job where I'd have to handle other people's bodily fluids as a matter of course. I don the gown, which is wildly flattering (not), and go to the bathroom.

As I sit on the toilet, I think about what this means. I know they want the pee because they are going to do a pregnancy test, a real one. Somewhere in the back of my mind, I've held out hope that the last test was defective. I mean, how accurate can a stick shoplifted from a convenience store in Bumfuck,

Nowhere, really be? But this? This is the real deal. If they say I'm pregnant, I'm pregnant.

I manage not to pee on my hand this time (I'm a fast learner) and leave the creepily warm cup on the back of the toilet. Then I go sit on the exam table and wait for Dr. Scapple and her instruments of torture. I peruse the various posters on the wall. One shows me the intricacies of my reproductive system. Another boasts fetuses in various stages of growth. I figure if I were pregnant, I would be about ten weeks pregnant. (Do you like the way I said "if I were"? I'm an eternal optimist.) According to the poster, my baby is about the size of a kumquat and looks like an alien with flippers.

Dr. Scapple enters the room. About five feet tall and pretty, she is not at all what I expected. Her black hair hangs almost to her waist. Her eyes shine. "They tell me you like to be called Harley," she says, beaming. I like her immediately. You must understand how rare this is. I like no one immediately. Hell, I like no one.

"Yeah, Harley is good," I say, taking her extended hand.

"And you knew when you came in that you were pregnant?" Her voice is gentle.

I nod. So the test was positive.

Dr. Scapple must guess that this isn't a happy situation for me because her eyes go soft. "Tough, huh?" she asks. When I went to see the doctor for chlamydia, she pursed her lips as she examined me and lectured me about using protection. I felt judged. But Dr. Scapple makes me want to put my head on her shoulder and cry. Blinking back tears, I nod.

"I'm so sorry," she says. "I'm going to do everything I can to help you, Harley, okay? First, I'll examine you, make sure you're healthy, and then, we'll talk about your options. I know this is scary, but remember, you have lots of choices. You aren't trapped."

As Dr. Scapple examines me, she talks good-naturedly about her two dogs and three cats. She almost makes me forget that the jaws of life are shoved up my hoo-hoo. Almost. Finally, she finishes. "Everything looks good," she says, removing her latex gloves. "Why don't you get dressed, and we'll go to my office and talk about your options."

I'm dizzy. It's real. I'm pregnant. Shouldn't I be in Mexico eating a worm from a tequila bottle or something? Not that I want to be. I mean, I've never been one of those girls who longs to sit on a beach slamming margaritas and flashing her boobs. But that sort of frivolity, idiotic as it may be, is infinitely preferable to going to a doctor's office to talk about my "options."

Dr. Scapple's office is cozy, decorated with bright colors. Pictures of the two dogs and three cats sit on her desk. A child's drawing—a sun and some flowers with a bunch of smiling stick figures—is taped to the wall. I wonder if Dr. Scapple has a kid. Seems like she would've mentioned it. Maybe not though. Maybe bringing up kids while examining pregnant hoo-hoos is bad medical form. I don't know. This whole routine is new to me.

Across the desk, Dr. Scapple takes off her glasses and scoots in her chair. "So before I begin, why don't you tell me a little about what's going on with you, Harley."

"Well, apparently I'm pregnant," I say, feeling foolish. Where should I start? With the pregnancy test? With Dean? With Mom's death? With my own birth?

She nods and smiles kindly. "That has to be overwhelming."

"Pretty much." I look at the kid's drawing. One of the people looks like Dr. Scapple, long, black Crayola pigtails.

"Is the father involved?" she asks.

"No." Instantly, I feel sorry because I'm making Dean look bad. "He would be if he could be," I add hastily. "But I don't want him to be right now."

"I understand," she says. "Sometimes, it's best to figure out what you're doing before you involve other people. How about your parents?"

"I don't know my dad," I say. "And my mom is dead."

"I'm so sorry to hear that," Dr. Scapple says, sounding genuinely sympathetic. "Is the loss recent?"

Damn it. I'm going to cry. "Yeah. About six months ago." I fight back tears.

Dr. Scapple reaches across the desk and grabs my hand. "You have a lot on your plate," she says.

"I thought picking a college was going to be my biggest challenge this year," I say, trying to make a joke of it. I start crying. "Damn." I swipe at my face. "I think these pregnancy hormones are getting to me."

"Maybe," says Dr. Scapple. "Or maybe you're just having a really hard time. Anyone would be overwhelmed in your situation. It's okay to cry."

So I do. Man, I mean, I turn on the waterworks. Dr.

Scapple keeps holding my hand while she tells me about my options. Keeping the baby. Putting it up for adoption. And getting an abortion. These are my choices. I pretty much knew that before I came here. But after sitting with Dr. Scapple for an hour, I feel way less alone. She gives me brochures full of information. Midwives in California. Adoption agencies. As I'm standing to leave, she hands me her card. "Call me if you need anything," she says. "Anything at all."

I pull away from the clinic. The sky seems brighter, tinged with hope, like the sky in the Old West paintings I see on the walls of every old place around here. There are always plains and grazing buffalo and a sun that is much more than a natural phenomenon exploding behind red cliffs, promising a life better than this one, a world where good things happen every day, a place where light transforms shadows to sparkle.

I gun the engine as I pull out on the freeway, and I ride.

⁓ℰ

Gravity and I never got along. If I had my druthers (that was something Mom used to say), I'd never touch the floor. Maybe Mercy's reincarnation theories are right, and I was a bird in a past life. I have a feeling I'd be way more at home in the sky than on the ground, which is why I love riding so much. Sure, I'm only a few feet above the earth, but it might as well be light-years. When I'm on my motorcycle, the road isn't pavement anymore. It's fast, celestial. It races by at warp speed, the way galaxies do in old *Star Trek* episodes.

Mom and I used to watch *Star Trek* religiously. She was mildly in love with Captain Picard and once followed a band based solely on the fact that they mentioned Jean-Luc in one of their songs. "Well, that, and the lead singer was a total hottie," she'd say when she talked about her groupie years. Her groupie years consisted of the ten or so concerts she attended while Mercy did babysitting duty, but whatever. She got Roger's (the hottie lead singer's) autograph and often reminisced about how he called her sweetheart. "Now there's a man I could've married," she'd say wistfully, staring at his photo on the cover of his CD. "Look at those eyes. Like fire."

"Jesus, Mom," I'd say, rolling my eyes. "Get a room."

Much to my dismay, she never took my admonitions to heart. If I had a penny for every Roger fantasy I had to hear, I'd be a rich woman. I'm being a smart ass, but I didn't really begrudge Mom her infatuation. Roger was Mom's only love while I was growing up. Her ghost lover, she called him. Maybe all she could handle was a ghost lover. I think my dad ruined her for all other men. Asshole.

Riding now, I shout-sing the Roger-song Mom used to love, the one about Jean-Luc.

I promise myself that for the rest of my life, I will sing Mom's song whenever I go to a new place to take her spirit with me. She always wanted to travel, but travel is difficult when you're a single mom. The most she could manage was our Saturday trips to the beach.

"Mom!" I yell, because the best thing about riding is no

one can hear you scream. "I will see everything! The pyramids! The Taj Mahal! The whole world! And you'll come with me!"

In a way, she will. She lives on in my DNA. I know enough about biology to understand this.

I think about the biology of the not-so-maybe-baby growing inside me. I wonder whose genes she got, if she will have my hair, if she will have Dean's eyes. And then I wonder why I used the pronoun "she" to describe it. Her. But I want to give her a pronoun, and I fall a little more in love with the baby in my belly, which seems to straddle a fine line between imaginary friend and human. Really, I guess right now she could be whatever I want her to be.

"She's a kumquat with flippers," I remind myself out loud.

A kumquat with flippers that is growing exponentially every day. A kumquat with flippers that needs to be dealt with ASAP. I want to keep riding, pretend this never happened, but if I don't handle her, she will handle me. If I thought having the jaws of life in my hoo-hoo sucked, I'd imagine having a for-sure baby pushing out of it would be worse. Way worse.

Up ahead, I see a sign for a bar. I'd tell you the actual name of the establishment, but if the sign is to be believed, it doesn't have one. It just says *BAR* in big black letters. It says something else above that, but it's so faded, I can't read it. The bar in question is a double-wide trailer set on concrete blocks. A makeshift porch hangs off the front like a tumor. Not exactly the Ritz-Carlton, but before I even know what I'm doing, I slow down. I don't know why. It's not like I'm old enough to drink. It's not like even if I was, I would be able to now, what with the kumquat sequestered in my uterus. But I pull over and go inside anyway. I want to talk to someone I don't know. More to the point, I want to talk to someone who doesn't know what a fuck-up I am. Which is unlike me. I rarely want to talk.

The one-roomed bar smells like stale beer and is empty except for a bunch of scarred tables, a few faded liquor posters featuring scantily clad women, and the bartender. I'll be damned if I'm going to add to the list of clichés I've become by spilling my guts to a bartender.

"Can I get you a drink?" he asks. His skin glows red in the light of a neon Budweiser sign. It doesn't seem like he is going to card me, and I'll tell you, were I not pregnant, I would so order a Long Island iced tea or a hurricane. Something with a reputation for getting people good and schnockered. But I am pregnant, so I say, "Just a Sprite," and take a stool at the bar.

He fills up a cup and sets it in front of me. "Not old enough to drink, huh?" he asks, winking.

"Nah," I say. "Not in public anyway."

"I figured, but I was going to let you off the hook. Give you whatever you asked for. Don't tell anyone."

I smile. "Thanks." Is he flirting with me? I think he's flirting with me.

"No problemo. I always make exceptions for pretty girls." He's definitely flirting with me. Now that he's flirting, I notice that he's kinda cute. Not in a loud "hey, check out my muscles, I work out ten hours a day" way, but more in a "hey, I probably forget to eat sometimes because I'm busy memorizing songs by the Cure, and if this was the eighties, I'd totally be sporting black eyeliner right now" way. Which is so my thing. He has one pierced eyebrow and a tattoo of an eagle on his forearm. His hair is jet-black and spiky. I finally notice his ratty-looking shirt says *Johnny Ramone* on it in tiny, faded letters. Not the Cure, but I was right about the decade.

I flirt back. "I always make exceptions for sexy guys and all that," I say, stirring my Sprite with my straw in a way that I hoped would seem seductive but, now that aforementioned stir is in progress, feels more awkward than anything.

My flirting sucks enough that he is rendered speechless. He shoves his hands into the pockets of his ratty jeans and grins.

I feel compelled to speak. (Mercy's waiting trick strikes again.) "So what's the tattoo for?"

"Which one?" he asks.

I nod to his forearm. "The only one I see."

"Oh, right. I forget people can't see my chest through my shirt." Perhaps for distraction, he pulls out a cloth and begins to wipe down the bar.

I stir my drink in that oh-so-sexy way again. "Well, I was trying not to let you in on my X-ray vision, at least until we got each other's names."

He smiles. "My name's Matt."

"I'm Harley."

"Kick-ass name, Harley. Now tell me about your X-ray vision."

When he grins this time, I notice he has this one crooked

tooth in the front, which does me in. You know how I feel about almost perfect teeth. I'm crushing on this kid hard-core.

"Tell me about your tattoos first."

He tosses the cloth under the bar. "Nope, X-ray vision is way more interesting than tattoos."

"Good point." It occurs to me that he is deflecting because he doesn't want to talk about his tattoos. I like him. I like anyone who uses my tricks. I lean forward as if I'm sharing a secret. "If you must know, it's pretty standard X-ray vision. As you might expect, I can see through things. For instance, I can tell you that you have a tattoo on your chest."

"Whoa," he says, miming shock. "What does my tattoo look like?"

"It's of something you don't want to talk about."

He seems a little surprised. "That's actually true," he says. "How did you know that?"

I shrug. "In addition to having X-ray vision, I'm also psychic."

"No way." His expression says he almost believes me. I consider continuing the ruse, but I feel sorry for him, standing there all hopeful, thinking I'm going to be able to tell him the day of his death or the first letter of the name of the woman he's destined to marry.

"I'm kidding," I say. "If people change the subject rapidly, it usually means they don't want to talk about the topic at hand. I know because I do it all the time."

"Why?" he asks.

"So this girl walks into a bar," I say.

He laughs. "Don't wanna talk about it, huh?"

I keep going. "And she sees this man sitting there drinking, looking really morose. There's this tiny man playing a miniature piano on the bar next to him."

Matt pulls a Dos Equis from the fridge. "Sure you don't want one?"

"I'm good."

"Do you mind if I have one?"

"Should you be drinking on the job?"

Matt flips off the lid. "Not technically, but my boss doesn't mind, and even if he did, he's never here anyway." He takes a swig. "So there's a tiny man playing the piano. Go on."

"Anyway, the girl walks to the dude and says, 'Hey, that's so cool. Where did you get that tiny musician?' The guy pulls a golden lamp out of his pocket, says, 'I used this. It's magic. I got three wishes. There are still two left if you want it.' The girl is blown away. 'Are you sure, dude? You're going to give me your magic lamp?' 'It's all yours,' says the guy. So the girl takes the lamp and says, 'I wish for a million bucks!' Immediately, a swarm of ducks flies into the room. They start pecking and shitting on everything. 'I said bucks! Not ducks!' screams the girl. The guy sitting at the bar looks at her. 'I shoulda mentioned the genie is deaf. What? You think I wished for a twelve-inch pianist?'"

Matt makes a noise that sounds like the deformed love child of a groan and a laugh. "Oh, god," he says. "That was worse than I thought it was going to be."

"It's all downhill from there," I say. "That's the best joke I have."

"Please don't tell me any more jokes."

"Then the only way we're going to fill the silence is if you tell me about your tattoos. I know you didn't want to talk about them, but I feel all subject matter is fair game now that we've bonded over foot-long pianists."

Matt thinks for a second. "Okay," he says. "Since we've bonded. The eagle is a tribute to my dad. He died last year in a hunting accident."

"That sucks big-time," I say. I can't believe he lost a parent too. If the crappy joke didn't bond us, this definitely does. "My mom died a few months ago so I totally get it."

"You're kidding," he says. "I'm so sorry."

"Actually, I'm driving to New York with her ashes." I try to sound nonchalant, but there is nothing that makes a person sound less nonchalant than trying to sound nonchalant. "So far, she's been a kinda shitty road tripping partner. Doesn't say much."

Matt seems to get my current need for gallows humor. "Maybe she's pissed. You taking her somewhere she'll like?"

"The beach where we used to play when I was a kid." I take a drink of my Sprite. It *really* doesn't take the edge off. I wish I could have a beer.

Matt touches his tattoo. "We spread Dad's ashes in his favorite stream. He was a fishing nut."

My phone buzzes. I pick it up and look at it. Mercy is calling.

"You need to get that?" asks Matt.

"Nah," I say, setting the phone on the bar. It would be shitty to interrupt Matt's personal revelation. "So why'd you get an eagle if your dad loved fishing?"

"He was a bird nut, too. Used to raise birds of prey. Hawks, eagles, owls."

"Isn't that illegal?"

"Yeah, but Dad didn't give a shit. I'm the only person I know who almost got eaten by a bald eagle when he was a baby."

I raise my eyebrows.

Matt laughs. "True story. Apparently, I was toddling in the yard, and my mom saw Dad's eagle swooping in to pick me up. She raced out and grabbed me right before the eagle did."

"Holy shit," I say.

"I know," he says. "Can you imagine how horrible that death would have been?"

Shuddering, I remember a painting of Prometheus having his liver ripped out by an eagle. "Wow. I should call you Prometheus Boy." As soon as I say this, I think of Dean, as until now, he was the only person I ever called _____ Boy. I remember the way he looked when I told him that he wasn't the maybe-baby's dad. Suddenly, I *need* a drink. Fuck it. One won't hurt, right? "You know what?" I say. "I changed my mind. I'll take you up on that beer."

Matt laughs. "I knew you'd cave. Dos Equis okay?"

"Mexican beer is the only beer I can stomach," I say. "Everything else tastes like shit." I'm trying to sound like I know about beer, but I'm actually parroting what Mom used to say. I have never tasted beer, probably because I've never been the kind of girl who gets invited to house parties when the cool kids' parents are out of town. My experiences with drinking are limited to my impromptu screw-top wine tastings with Amy, my clandestine raids of Mercy's liquor cabinet, and those bottles of bourbon I shared Dean. One of them ended in pregnancy, so it's fair to say my drinking with a cute boy would probably be a really bad idea even if I wasn't pregnant. But I take the Dos Equis Matt hands me and throw it back anyway. It tastes better than liquor. Think drinking water-downed urine, as opposed to drinking rubbing alcohol. You must have decided by now that I am the queen of shitty ideas—and an amoral asshole. And maybe I am. I don't know anymore. I have no idea who I am or why I do the things I do.

Six months ago, I could have told you exactly who I was. I was a secretly badass English nerd who was probably going to be a lawyer. I was going to meet some not-so-nice boy in law school, marry him, and have one, maybe two kids. After that, I was going to get rich and buy my mom a house so she would never have to work again. But now? My life plan has been derailed. I expected a walk through the park, and life sent me to survival camp in the desert. All I know for sure is that while I sit here at this bar, drinking beer with Matt, laughing at the shitty jokes he tells me, the tornado inside me quiets to a dull hum. I barely even notice it's there.

I'm four beers in when my phone dings. I pick it up, thinking Mercy is texting. She has already called three times. But it's not Mercy. It's Dean. Can we talk?

I stare at the text. Matt's saying something about baseball.

As I remember the way Dean's skin felt, I don't care what Matt has to say. I start to text back. Yeah, I fucking miss you. My phone changes "fucking" to "ducking."

"Who ever wanted to type the word ducking?" I ask Matt.

He laughs. "Auto-correct inserting barnyard animals into your text?"

I nod.

"At least it isn't inserting a million ducks into the bar."

I stare at him blankly. "Huh?"

"Your crappy joke?" he prompts. "The ducks and the foot-long pianist?"

"Oh, yeah." I smile politely.

"Attempt at humor officially failed," he says. He grins again. Damn, I love that tooth.

I press Delete. "You're telling me." I finish my fourth bottle of beer in one gulp.

~ℰ~

What happens next is pretty much a blur. Suffice it to say that while Matt is cute and charming and funny, by the end of the night, he has sufficiently reminded me that there are more boys like the Asshole in the world than there are boys like Dean.

These are the facts, as I remember them:

1. The night grew dark. A storm gathered. (Insert ominous theme music here.) Matt declared me incapable of driving, especially in the rain.

2.   I insisted I would stay in the bar until I was sober.

"I have to close the bar," Matt said.

I checked my phone again and saw another text from Dean. I don't know if this makes me an asshole, but I still love you, it said.

"The sign on the door says you're open until midnight. It's only eight," I said to Matt.

"I close early when there are no customers," he replied.

"I'm a customer."

"Not a customer that counts."

I wasn't sure what he meant by that, but even as drunk as I was, I could tell it probably wasn't good. There was something vaguely not-nice simmering in Matt's eyes. I remember it only retrospectively. At the time, I noticed it and then explained it away. *You're being paranoid,* I told myself.

3.   I said I was going to drive to a hotel. Matt said if I tried, he was obligated to call the cops, which was probably true, but I started to wonder if he was worried about my safety or trying to get me alone.

"Are you joking?" I asked.

"No," he answered.

I still wasn't sure if he was joking.

4.   I said I was going to get a cab. Matt asked where I thought I was. New York City? I thought for sure he

was joking that time because he smiled. I noticed that crooked tooth again. It didn't seem a fraction as cute as it had before.

5. Matt offered to drive me "somewhere safe." Feeling as if I was out of options, and being drunk enough to ignore the alarm bells that were going off in my brain, I remembered how pleasant he'd been all evening, I told myself I was being a drama queen, and I asked him to take me to the nearest hotel. (Side note: NEVER ignore alarm bells.) I climbed into his silver piece of shit car. It smelled like he smoked in there 24–7 with the windows shut. Did I mention I hate the smell of cigarettes? I was pretty sure I was getting lung cancer simply sitting in that rolling death trap.

6. On the way to somewhere safe, which seemed to be conveniently located in the middle of nowhere, Matt pulled over on the side of the road. A water tower loomed in the distance, and a group of cows milled around in a field nearby. Those were the only signs of civilization as far as the eye could see. The sound of the windshield wipers slapping sounded sinister.

"You're super hot," Matt said. Lightning flashed in the distance, and I almost wanted to laugh at Mother Nature's timing, adding ominous natural phenomenon to the twisting warning feeling in my gut.

I was suddenly less drunk.

"I'm gonna go," I said, reaching for the door handle.

"Where?" he asked. "To hang out with the cows in the rain?" He pushed a button, and the automatic locks clicked into place. My skin went cold with dread. I know what you're thinking. How did this nice guy turn into such a dick? Or at least that's what I was thinking. I'm quickly learning that dicks almost always masquerade as nice guys. No one ever approaches you and says, "Hey, I'm a dick. Wanna hang out?"

Matt leaned in to kiss me. I backed away. "Dude, unlock my door."

He smiled. That crooked tooth was decidedly not appealing. Whatever the opposite of cute is, that's what that tooth was. Revolting? Chilling? Gag inducing? "Come on. Kiss me."

"No."

Matt insisted. And by insisted, I mean pushed me up against the window and stuck his tongue down my throat. His hands on my shoulders were hard and cold. They hurt. His mouth tasted like the car smelled. How did he taste like smoke when he hadn't smoked in the past few hours? Was his flesh permanently saturated with nicotine?

Detour: things you should know about me. As I mentioned, Mom paid for me to take martial arts classes the whole time I was growing up. She didn't want me to ever be in a position where I couldn't defend myself. When Matt kissed me against my will, those muted alarm bells started screaming. And thirty seconds later, when he stuck his hand up my shirt, my reptilian brain took over. You know the brain they say comes out to play when you're drunk, the one that acts on instinct, not logic? Well, mine happens to be saturated with martial arts. Long story short, I broke cute little Matt's nose with the heel of my hand, reached over him to unlock the doors, got out of the car, made my jacket into a sort of tent to protect my head and phone from the rain, and called 911, all in less than a minute. Lest he get any ideas about chasing me, I screamed, "I'm calling 911, asshole!" while dialing. His taillights disappeared before the operator said, "911. What is your emergency?"

"I got in a fight with my boyfriend, and he dropped me in the middle of a freaking field. I need to get back to town."

"Where are you?"

"I have no idea. There's a water tower."

"Okay. By the tower. I'll have a unit there in ten minutes."

I hung up, stunned that there were places in the world where your location could be precisely determined by the proximity of a water tower.

7.   A cop came and picked me up. She didn't make me ride in the back like a criminal, which I appreciated. Her hair was wrapped around her head in a tight braid that reminded me of a traditional Dutch girl. As we were driving, she glanced at me, seeming to know something was very wrong.

"You all right?" she asked. I didn't tell her about Matt's nose. I didn't tell her how he stuck his hand up my shirt and the horror I felt when his dirty, clammy skin touched parts of me I didn't let anyone see. I didn't tell her that if my mom hadn't gotten me those classes, I might have ended up raped, or worse—dead in Matt's car.

"I'm fine," I said.

"You have blood on your shirt," she pointed out.

"Oh, yeah. I had a bloody nose. Too much picking in the dry heat, I guess."

If you want someone to change the subject, start talking about picking your nose. At least that was my theory, but the cop kept going.

"You look like you've been crying."

"My boyfriend is a dick. And I miss my mom. She died recently."

"I'm sorry, honey," she said.

Sorry, sorry, sorry. Everyone is sorry. What a fucking useless word. It can't bring Mom back. It can't make me not pregnant. It can't do anything. It's like a penny. You can't buy shit with it.

"Thanks," I said.

"Thanks for nothing" seemed like too much of a cliché, so I didn't say it out loud.

TEN

I t's 4:56 a.m., approximately seven hours after the cop dropped me off at the Majestic Plains Inn. Shockingly, the rooms are not as luxurious as the term "majestic" implies, unless you consider vibrating beds built in circa 1972 a luxury. Yes, my accommodations boast a vibrating bed. No, I don't use the vibrating feature, not for lack of desire, but for lack of quarters.

I still haven't slept, mostly because I keep reaching for my purse and digging for change (I really want to experience the vibrating bed while I have the chance), but also because what happened with Matt is eating at me. Also, did I mention I'm pregnant and hungover? (I'm keenly cognizant those two words should never appear in the same sentence.)

It was hot when I got to my room, so I turned on the air full blast. It's freezing now. I guess I could get up and turn on the heat, but I want to stay huddled under the blankets wearing Mom's jacket, a Bob Marley T-shirt, and ratty jeans. Also a pair of toe socks Mom gave me. She bought me weird socks every year for Christmas. It was our thing. These have frogs on them. I happened to be wearing them the night of the fire. I don't know why I keep wearing them now. It should make me sad, and it does, but it feels like a piece of her. If I let go of the physical evidence she was here, she *really* stops existing, right?

Mom loved frogs because they had "fat eyes," which was the term she used to describe anything that had big, kind eyes. According to her, all dogs, deer, and frogs had fat eyes. Also some aliens, but only the benevolent ones like E.T. Not the ones that anal probed people. She also described me as having fat eyes. I didn't like it at the time, but I'd give anything to have her sitting next to me, telling me about my fat eyes. "I don't mean it in a bad way," she'd say. "There are some concepts human language can't capture. Fat eyes is one of them."

"If there were a word for 'fat eyes,' what would it be?" I asked her.

We were sitting at a vegan restaurant when we had this conversation. A giant mural of Ganesh hung over Mom's head. Mom was eating tofu curry. I don't know why I remember that, but I do. I can't tell you what I ate that night.

"I just said there is no word."

"I know. Make one up."

She thought for a minute, her chopsticks frozen in midair. "I can't convey the concept with words, but I could totally express it through the art of interpretative dance," she finally said, setting her chopsticks on the table.

"Don't you dare," I whispered.

She was already moving her chair and standing up. Some new-agey music involving flutes and bells was playing, and she commenced gyrating and swiveling her hips.

"Mom, sit down!" I ordered. "People are staring."

She only danced harder, seemingly oblivious to the other diners' disapproval. As much as Mom humiliated me sometimes, I had to give her kudos for not giving a shit what anyone thought of her. Mom was Mom. No apologies.

I started to laugh. "You are such a dumb ass! What does this have to do with fat eyes anyway?"

She laughed too, delighted I had found her antics amusing. Mom was like a little kid doing tricks at a pool. *Clap for me! Tell me how cute I am!* I loved her for that. "Fat eyes are like the eyes Hindu gods have. Benevolent. Divine. Beautiful." She pointed to the Ganesh painting. "He has fat eyes."

"And this relates to you having seizures how?"

She slumped into her chair, defeated. "I was *not* having seizures! I was belly dancing."

"That was belly dancing?"

"Everyone's a critic." She picked up her chopsticks and started eating again.

"Okay, let's pretend for a minute that was belly dancing. I still don't get how it relates to fat eyes."

"Hindu gods belly dance."

"They so don't," I said.

"They do too. Ask Mercy."

Mercy was the all-knowing oracle we called upon to decide disputes regarding spirituality.

A whoosh of freezing air brings me back to the present. Since Mercy is now on my mind, I pick up my phone from the nightstand and hit Mercy's number. I texted her when I got to the hotel to let her know I was safe. I didn't tell her about Matt because I didn't want to talk about him. Or anything. But now, I'm ready to talk. It rings.

"Hello," she says. I can tell I woke her up. She sounds grumpy, but her voice still makes me feel less cold.

"Hey, I have a question," I say.

"Okay." I can almost see her rubbing the sleep out of her eyes, arranging her features into a patient expression even though she wants to kill me for calling so early.

"Do Hindu gods belly dance?"

In my imagination, her benevolent expression evaporates. "You seriously woke me up at three o'clock to ask me that?" Shit. I forgot about the time difference.

"Mom said they do."

"Oh." (She's donning the kind expression again, realizing this is about me missing Mom.) "Well, I regret to inform you that your mother was full of shit."

"I knew it."

"Having a hard morning, kid? I was worried about you last night."

I roll over. "Yeah, sorry. I wasn't ready to talk." I

contemplate telling her about Matt, then think better of it. She will be horrified that I drank while pregnant. Hell, I'm horrified. "I went to Planned Parenthood like we discussed."

"Good! What happened?"

"I saw a doctor. She said I'm for sure pregnant and stuck the jaws of life up my hoo-hoo."

She laughs. "The jaws of life?"

"I swear, Mercy. You should have seen these things. Vicious metal mandibles the size of a crane."

"I've seen them. I've been to the gynecologist before."

"Me too, but I'm pretty sure since my last visit, the gynecological association ruled to replace regular speculum with T-rex-sized instruments of torture. I thought for sure there had been car wreck in my vagina. Little people pinned in there screaming 'Help!'"

"You're a freak." I can hear Mercy smiling.

"You have no idea." I say it like I'm joking, but I'm not. I mentally compose a list of my most recent freakish acts.

Harley's Heinous Deeds (Senior Year Edition):

1. Killing my mom (that's a doozy)
2. Getting sloshed and fucking my best friend
3. Getting pregnant by aforementioned best friend
4. Kicking my best friend out of my life even though he's the second nicest person I've ever known
5. Drinking while pregnant
6. Putting myself in a situation where I could have gotten raped

"Your freakishness is one of my favorite things about you," Mercy says. I hear dishes banging. She must be making coffee.

I picture Mercy's kitchen, wishing I was there now. "Yay! I have a fan club of two, and one of them is dead."

"Your mom is still in the universe, loving you like always."

I've never believed Mercy's platitudes, but I want to believe this one. My throat gets tight. I stare up at the water-stained ceiling, trying not to cry.

"In any case," Mercy continues, "I'm a pretty cool fan club. One of me is better than ten other humans."

"I wouldn't go that far."

The banging stops. The coffee must be brewing. "Do you have any idea what you're going to do, Harley? Whatever it is, I'll support you. You know that."

It's just what Mom would have said. No wonder they were friends. "I'm not ready to be a mom, Mercy. Some shit happened, and, well, I don't even think I could be trusted with a hamster right now."

"Are you still going to Omaha?"

"Maybe. I don't know. I think I'm going back to Planned Parenthood first."

I didn't know that was what I was thinking, but when I say it out loud, I realize it's a good idea. The best I can come up with anyway. If I can't even make it through my first trimester without doing something that could seriously fuck up my baby forever, how can I possibly be expected to behave like a decent parent for eighteen whole years?

I make an appointment, and the next day, I go back to the clinic, this time to get an abortion. Because life is determined to treat me like a walking cliché, there *is* a protestor on the sidewalk when I arrive at Planned Parenthood. Just one, but this sucker is big. Six feet tall, give or take. He has a bald spot roughly the size of Texas, which he has attempted to disguise by styling his three remaining strands of wispy hair into a fetching comb-over. He's holding a sign that says ABORTION IS MURDER. I try to get inside before he sees me, but he jogs over as I open the door, glaring at me like I'm Satan.

"Abortion stops a beating heart," he says, shoving a pamphlet at me.

I don't take it. "So does a revolver." I nod at my boot, trying to look like a girl who may or may not be packing a pistol in her footwear.

"Is that a threat?" he asks, stunned.

"Nah, just an attempt at conversation."

"Get away from the door!" the receptionist yells from inside. "Or I'm calling the police." She stands and starts to walk toward us. Mr. Comb-Over backs away.

Trying not to look as scared as I feel, I rush into the clinic, grateful to hear the door close behind me.

"I'm so sorry about that," the receptionist says. "Are you okay?"

I nod even though I'm nothing close to okay. I can barely breathe through the lump in my throat. Still, I don't cry until a few minutes later. When the tears finally come, I'm lying on a table wearing my frog socks and a flimsy gown that hides nothing important. The sheet of paper between me and the metal table does little to mitigate the cold. Mopping my eyes, I try to focus on the kumquat with flippers. "Sorry, maybe-baby," I whisper. "Mercy says we reincarnate. Next time around, you'll do better. You don't need a shit mom like me."

I know it can't hear me. I know it is nothing but fetal tissue right now. But still, it must have a soul, right? I mean, if all living things have souls, surely my maybe-baby has one too. Maybe not a fully developed one like me, but a kumquat-size soul.

"Hello, Harley." Dr. Scapple's voice is gentle as she enters the room wearing scrubs.

"Hi," I say, watching her walk toward me, thinking she's way prettier than I gave her credit for the first time I saw her. She takes my hand and squeezes it. Her fingers are so warm.

"How you holding up?" Her gray eyes are kind, surrounded with wrinkles like suns ringed by rays. I suddenly get what Mom meant by "fat eyes."

"I'm scared," I whisper.

"I know," she says. "It's okay to be scared."

"Do you think my baby will hate me?"

She sweeps a strand of hair away from my face and tucks it behind my ear, like Mom would have done. This makes me cry harder. "Nobody is going to hate you, Harley. You are a good person making an incredibly difficult decision. No one has the right to judge you."

"I'm not a good person."

She smiles. "Yes, you are."

"How do you know?"

"I can tell by your eyes."

I laugh. "Do you think I have fat eyes too?"

"What?" she asks.

"It's something my mom used to say."

"It sounds like you really loved her."

"So much."

"Well, if she was here, what would she say?" Dr. Scapple asks me.

I look away from her and stare at an ocean sunset taped to the ceiling. "She'd tell me to follow my heart."

"And what does your heart say?"

I must be quiet for a long time because Dr. Scapple finally says, "Harley?"

"I'm not sure," I whisper.

Dr. Scapple is silent for a minute. Finally, she says, "It sounds as if the question isn't whether your baby is going to hate you. The question is whether *you* are going to hate you. Are you sure this is what you want?"

I look up at the sunset again, studying the dying daylight seeping into the sea. I think about Mom and the beach. Closing my eyes, I picture us there together. I remember the words she used to whisper to me: *But soft, what light from yonder window breaks? It is the east, and Juliet is the sun.*

What if this baby is my sun the way I was Mom's? What if she is my home, and I don't know it yet? Or what if Mercy is right? What if we do reincarnate, and this baby is Mom in a new body? I remember the way I felt on the freeway when I was about to kill myself. Knowing my maybe-baby was there saved me. This seems like a truly shitty way to return the favor.

I open my eyes and look at Dr. Scapple. She smiles encouragingly.

"I don't think I can do this," I say.

ELEVEN

By the time I reach Omaha, Dean has texted me again. Look, I can take a hint, and I'd totally leave you alone if you weren't pregnant with a baby that is possibly mine. But under the circumstances, I can't fuck off. Will you please call me?

I want to write back, but I don't know what to say to him, so I say nothing, which is probably a terrible decision. I try not to imagine him sitting in his bedroom staring at the *Star Wars* posters on the walls (Dean is a huge geek) wondering what the hell he did to deserve this treatment from his Princess Leia.

"Yoda, your help I need," I mumble to myself as I pull into a parking lot on the outskirts of Omaha.

It's a prayer of some kind, I suppose. Like I said, I don't believe in god, but I'm desperate enough to pray anyway. I'd be rubbing a lucky rabbit's foot if I had one. Anything that might sway the universe to be nicer to me. I feel way more comfortable praying to Yoda than I do any traditional god, and I kinda figure any god worth his salt isn't going to get hung up on a nickname. What bugs me about religion is it's so petty. I mean, if I decided to call Mercy "home slice," she wouldn't stop being my friend. But this deity in the sky is supposed to torture you for all eternity if you get his name wrong? I want nothing to do with that version of god.

I yank off my helmet and look around. The way Mom talked about Omaha, I thought it would be like Oz. But Omaha is the anti-Oz. It's only interesting if you're into strip malls and cow sculptures. I'm not.

At a sidewalk café nearby, a small boy plays with a truck while his mother eats a salad. He makes *vroom* noises and crashes his toy into a ketchup bottle. It tips over, squirting a bit of ketchup onto his mother's blouse. She must be a saint because her only reaction is to pick up a napkin, dip it in her ice water, and dab at the red blob. I can't imagine myself responding quite so benignly. Nor can imagine myself wearing a blouse.

"Hank, eat your lunch, honey," the mother says.

"*Vrrrrooooommmmm,*" says Hank. He sends his truck careening into the saltshaker. It clatters to the ground.

His mother bends to pick it up. "Hank, your lunch."

Clearly, he's not interested in the grilled cheese sandwich in front of him. It remains untouched on his plate. His mother takes the truck from him, gently saying, "You can have it back when you finish half of your sandwich."

Hank looks at her like he's considering matricide. In

lieu of beating her to death with the mustard, he picks up a potato chip and flings it at a flock of pigeons nearby. Pecking at one another, they scramble for the prize. Bolstered by their response, Hank lifts another chip and tosses it. The feathered crowd goes wild.

His mother does not approve. "Don't give the birds your lunch, buddy. Eat it."

Hank picks up an apple slice and holds it in the air, a missile poised for launch.

"Hank!" A warning.

Hank throws the slice at her. It gets caught in her soccer mom hairdo. I picture myself sporting a highlighted bob perpetually decorated with food. As I pull on my helmet, Hank launches into a screeching tantrum. His mother goes to him. The last thing I see in my rearview is Hank's mother attempting to restrain him while he kicks her in the stomach.

Awesome.

When I'm freaked out, I take the corners faster than I should. Somehow, translating my internal terror to actual danger stabilizes my emotions. Sometimes. But in spite of my foray into reckless driving, I can't stop seeing Hank's poor mother desperately holding on to his feet as he practices his best kickboxing moves on her. Seriously? I have one of these tyrannical creatures growing inside me? I'll be lucky to live through two years with one of those in the house. The first time I confiscate a toy, *whack!* The kid karate-chops me to kingdom come. I seriously question my decision not to have an abortion.

When my freak-out abates, leaving dull terror in its place, I pull into another parking lot and run a search on my phone for "Los Milagros."

"Let's get this over with," I mutter. I've been in Omaha for all of twelve minutes, and I'm already desperate to get the hell out. According to my GPS, Mom's famed jewelry store is 2.6 miles away. I drive.

I don't know what I expected from Los Milagros, but I'm pretty sure this isn't it. It's situated in a strip mall between a nail salon and a check-cashing place. The sign, boasting several red roses and a dove, is faded. Through the windows, I see an old lady hunched over the counter reading. I wonder if that's Mom's fabled "otherworldly" woman. There are no customers.

Feeling silly for thinking I could have some kind of epiphany in a jewelry store, I consider driving away. I mean, look at this shit hole. It's almost certainly not going to deliver the experience I had in mind. Sure, if this were a movie, I would walk in and find a magic amulet, and my path would become clear. Music would swell, and I would walk back out the door a Hallmark commercial instead of an after-school special. But this isn't a movie. This is real life. And as far as I can tell, real life is way better dealing out questions than it is answers. Still, leaving after I've come all this way feels stupid, so I get off my bike and go in.

"Hello," the woman at the counter says as I enter. She closes her book, a tattered copy of *The Collected Poems of Octavio Paz*. At least she has good taste in literature.

"Hi," I say, looking around. The walls are hung with

various pieces of jewelry, all of them breathtaking. A turquoise moon pendant catches my eye. I go to it, turning it over and admiring the intricate silver rays surrounding the moon's blue center. Mercy would love it. "This is incredible."

"Thank you." She smiles, sweeping a strand of gray hair away from her face, which is quite beautiful in spite of her age. She must be pushing seventy, but her eyes shine like a child's. Her voice carries faint traces of a Mexican accent.

"You made it?" I ask.

She sweeps her hand around the store. "I made all of this. It is in my blood, jewelry making. It was my mother's work, and now it is mine."

"You're good. Have you always owned this store?" I turn the moon over again, trying to act casual.

"For the last thirty years," she says.

My heart pounds. So this is the woman who sold Mom the necklace. It's weird to meet a legend from your childhood. I feel nervous, like I'm talking to Elvis or some long-gone, larger-than-life ghost. It might be creepy to tell her how much my mom talked about her, so instead, I hold up the pendant and ask, "How much?"

"How much can you afford?" she asks.

I smile. "Are you serious? You don't set prices?"

She smooths her colorful skirt. "Well, I do, but they are subject to change for people I like."

"How do you know you like me?"

"I am a *curandera*. We know things."

"What's a curandera?"

"A medicine woman. Back in Mexico, healing was also my mother's work. She passed this along to me too."

So she's a witch, I think, wondering if she has a stash of eye of newt in the storeroom. "What kind of stuff do you know?" I ask.

"I know you have guts."

One thing is certain: she is *not* psychic in any way. I want to tell her she's nuts. If only she had seen me curled up blubbering in my hotel room a few nights ago. "I'm not sure about that," I say. "I'm scared all the time." I don't know why I confess that to her. Maybe because I will never see her again. Maybe because she feels more like a myth than a person to me. Maybe because I want to show her that all of her assumptions about me are wrong. Maybe all of the above.

"It's not brave if you're not scared," she says. She taps the book. "He called women like you 'bright stars.'"

I recognize the phrase immediately. It's from a poem called "No More Clichés," about the difference between physical beauty and inner beauty, and frankly, it kicks ass. I wrote an essay about it. I could have an intellectual discourse about it if I wanted to. I could display what I know. But I *don't* want to. I don't like people who use their knowledge of literature to show off. To me, it's sacred. I like to keep it in my heart, private, kind of like my pain. "I'm not much of a bright star. More of a dusty one at the moment." I look down at my sweaty clothes and laugh.

"Your eyes shine," she tells me.

I freeze, remembering Dr. Scapple saying she could see I

was a good person by looking at my eyes. "I can't believe you said that."

"Why?"

"You are the second person who said so today. It's weird. My mom used to tell me that all the time."

"Used to?" she asks.

"Yeah, she died." Before she can tell me how sorry she is, I go to her and set the moon necklace on the counter. "Will you take one hundred dollars?"

"Too much," she says.

I shake my head. "You know you're haggling in the wrong direction, right? You're supposed to tell me it's worth more than that."

"But it's not," she says matter-of-factly.

"Still," I say. "I want to pay you that much." I take out a hundred-dollar bill and set it on the counter. "This money was left to me when my mom died, and your store was really important to her. To us. It's kinda a tribute to her."

"Who was your mother?" she asks. "Did I know her?"

"Probably not." I reach behind me and unclasp Mom's necklace. "You made this for her years ago. I'm sure you don't remember."

She picks up the pendant and runs her leathery fingers over it, her brow creased. Finally, she grins and says, "Ah, yes! I remember!"

I'm stunned. "You're kidding."

"No, I'm not kidding." Her eyes tear up. I'm a little freaked out by the intensity of her reaction. "I remember your mother well. One of the most beautiful souls every to pass through my store. And her story. So sad. You found her then?"

I'm confused. "Well, yeah. She was my mom. Kinda hard to miss her."

For some weird reason, she looks stunned. "She didn't give you up?"

"Give me up?" I ask, completely flummoxed.

"Never mind," she says, wiping at her eyes. "Yes, such a pretty piece. And your mother was a lovely girl."

"What did you mean 'give me up'?"

She reaches out and touches my hand, seeming to weigh her thoughts. Finally, she says, "*Majita*, would you like the ugly truth or a pretty lie?"

My stomach flip-flops. "The ugly truth," I whisper. Instinctively, I understand I'm stepping off a cliff I will never come back from. I consider changing my answer to "a pretty lie," but I don't.

"I knew you had guts," she says. Warmth from her hand seeps into mine. "I can tell you do not know the whole story. I can also tell you need to know. So I will tell you. When your mother came to me, she was pregnant with you. She didn't think she could raise you, so she was giving you to a couple that wanted a baby very much. She asked me to make a necklace for them to give to you on your eighteenth birthday. She was going to write you a letter to go with it. She hoped you'd come looking for her."

I stare at the woman. "You must be thinking of someone else," I say. "My mom never wanted to put me up for adoption. I was her home. She said she knew it the moment I was inside her."

"Of course," she says. "Yes. I'm thinking of someone else. You're right."

But I can tell she's lying. My throat tightens. Struggling to maintain my composure, I grab my mother's necklace and shove it in my pocket. Then I push the moon necklace toward her. "Can I pay for this?"

"You take it," she insists. "It's a gift."

"No," I say, trying to be all business. "A deal is a deal." I slide the hundred-dollar bill across the counter and turn toward the door.

"*Majita!*" she calls after me.

I don't look back. I don't want to cry in front of her, and I will if I look at her again.

"Your mother loved you very much. Sometimes the best things come when we aren't ready for them. Sometimes roses bloom in the desert."

I want to say something—anything—but the words get caught in my throat. I nod and keep on walking.

TWELVE

That fucking store. Los Milagros, my ass. More like Los Shit Tacos. Driving out of Omaha, I laugh at my bad joke, because I've cried enough on this trip. I'm so stupid. What did I think was going to happen? Did I think Mom was going to manifest among the earrings and tell me what to do with my maybe-baby? Whatever I thought was going to happen, I sure as hell did not expect to find out my mom didn't want me. I must be driving shittily because a guy in a truck honks at me. I flip him the bird.

My mom was going to put me up for adoption. Everything she ever told me about who I was, where I came from, was a lie. I want to hurl her ashes over a bridge, walk away from her, never speak to her again. But petty tantrums are pointless, as she isn't here to be affected by my rage. With or without my approval, she will never talk to me again. "Fuck you, Mom!" I scream. My words blow back in my face, sounding garbled. That doesn't stop me from shouting them again.

I think about calling Mercy to talk through this, but I feel betrayed by her too. She must have known, right? Why didn't she tell me? Why didn't anyone tell me? "Fuck you, Mercy!" I yell.

I squeeze my bike with my knees, as if it's the last reliable thing I have to hold on to. A storm brews in the distance. Sooty clouds hang heavy over endless plains. Jagged lightning tears them once, twice, three times in just as many seconds. I wonder why the ferocious bolts don't explode the sky. I wonder why the earth doesn't go up in flames. I watch the electric carnage, thinking it feels right, mimicking the way I feel inside. How many times can I be torn before I rip in half forever? Again, I wonder if I am on some reality TV show where the producers hurl shit-situation after shit-situation at contestants to see if they will crack. "You win!" I scream at the imaginary producers. "I give up, okay? Uncle!"

Thunder booms. I wonder if god is responding, if Yoda is replying, if whatever the hell is out there is communicating with me. "I'm glad I have your attention!" I yell. "You took my mom, you asshole! I hate you!"

A few raindrops splatter on my face. I lick my lips, loving the taste of them, feeling for the first time in a long time that I am connected to something that isn't me. For better or for worse, I'm talking to this storm.

"Did you hear me? I hate your guts!" I shout. God is done toying with me. Rain falls fiercely in thick, stinging sheets. Just when I think I will have to pull over, I see a sign that says HOLY FAMILY SHRINE.

Most days, this sign would elicit a dismissive snicker from me at best, a blasphemous pun at worst. So why do I go there now? Why do I do anything I do? Why did I sleep with Dean? Why did I almost get an abortion? Why did I go into that hellhole jewelry store? I suppose because I'm doing my best to follow Mom's highway of diamonds, except figuring out which step shines is way harder than she let on. I suppose because I'm willing to overturn any and all stones, looking for answers. But under every rock I upend, I find another question. Still, I have to keep looking, or I may go insane.

So while I follow the signs pointing to the shrine, suffice it to say that I don't have high hopes. I drive the unpaved roads, mud splattering my boots and jeans. My already paltry expectations fade to nothing when I find out that the grassland near the hill where the shrine is situated is inhabited by cows.

"Nothing says holy quite like a herd of cattle," I mumble, realizing only after I say it that my statement would be considered accurate in India and ancient Egypt. In America, however, cows don't mean sacred. Cows mean lunch.

I pull into the shrine's parking lot. It's empty. The rain has abated, and as I dismount, water drips from flowering bushes lining the path to the shrine. The world smells new. Drenched and shivering, I climb the rocky trail, watching bees dart and long grasses sway. When I reach the top, the sight of the shrine stops me cold. It's like no church I've ever seen. Composed almost entirely of glass, it acts as a prism, reflecting and refracting the red rays of the setting sun. In spite of myself, I catch my breath, hardly believing its ethereal beauty. Hesitantly, I walk toward the church and pull on the door. It's locked. I can see rough-hewn benches inside. There's an altar, but no priests. I am alone and apparently barred from entering the sanctuary. Probably to be expected considering I just screamed "I hate you" in god's face.

I'm not sure that I'm disappointed. I do well with solitude. It's my thing. My encounters with other humans almost always seem to end in catastrophe. As for church services? Well, you can guess how I feel about that.

I turn away from the doors, wondering what to do now. The trail I walked to get here continues past the shrine. I start to walk again.

As I shuffle along the trail, quiet swallows me. It feels more profound than physical silence. It feels like peace. The storm inside me dies down. Ahead, a giant gray rock looms. When I step around it, I find a life-size statue of the Virgin Mary standing at the center of a rocky enclosure. She's pure white stone. The ground beneath her feet is dotted with flowers, along with a small marker engraved with the words, "Perfect love casts out all fear."

I sink onto the bench in front of her, finding myself moved by her beauty in spite of my decidedly irreligious leanings. Her face is gentle, and were she human, I imagine she would be the perfect mother. Loving. Accepting. A great listener. Kinda like the mom I used to have. Kinda like my very own Mary. As I realize her resemblance to Mom, I start to cry. Again. And I know by now you probably think I'm just a big wuss, but I'm not. Until my mom died, I almost never cried. Now, I never stop.

I make a split-second decision, the kind of unfounded, impulsive choice I've been making ever since I found myself living in a world that didn't have my mother in it. I pretend the Virgin Mary is Mom.

"Momma," I whisper. My voice sounds childlike, broken. I'm so glad no one is here to hear me. I imagine the statue cocks her head a tiny bit to listen. "I'm pregnant, just like you were. I don't know what to do. No matter what choice I make, it's going to rip me apart. I know this maybe-baby is just a fetus. Still, I already love it."

The sun drops behind the horizon, and purple twilight falls. I stay quiet for a while, listening to the chirping of crickets and the lowing of cows in the distance. After a few minutes, I go on. "I can't raise this kid. I'm not ready to get kicked by tyrannical, tantrum-throwing, apple-tossing demon spawn. And Mom. I got drunk the day after I found out. Seriously? Did anyone ever teach me about fetal alcohol syndrome? Yes, they did, but I did it anyway because I'm the worst person who ever lived."

The moon gleams yellow. A night bird sings. Mary keeps listening. "I'm so alone. I've never been so alone. Before you died, I thought I understood loneliness when people were mean to me. But I would run to you, and there you'd be, waiting with your shitty banana cookies—sorry, Mom, I only choked them down to make you happy. You'd hold me and tell me everything was okay, and I knew there was no way I'd ever be lost. You told me I was your home every day, but, Momma, I don't think I ever told you that you were mine. And now, I'm homeless. And people are as mean as they ever were. I'm as big a freak as I ever was. Only these days, I have no place to run. There are no shitty banana cookies waiting for me anywhere."

Drops of water plop on my hands, which are folded in my lap, clutching each other for dear life. I don't know if they are tears or raindrops, and I don't care. I stare at the Virgin Mary, and maybe it's my imagination, but I feel warmth wrap around me, soft and good. Perfect love. What I felt when Mom gave me those shitty banana cookies. "You aren't the worst person in the world," it says. "Sure, you suck, but have you ever heard of Hitler?" I laugh because whether it's my imagination or Mom, this is exactly the kind of thing she would have said to make me smile and forget for just a minute how vicious life can be.

"I can't believe you didn't want me," I say.

The warmth makes me feel wanted, and I somehow understand that eighteen years ago, my mom was me, a willful girl driving across the country with a belly full of maybe-baby, trying to figure out what the hell to do. I can't be mad at her because I know how scary it is to be me. "I get it, Mom," I say. "Even if you didn't know I was your home when you first knew I was inside you, you were always, always a home for me. I'll love you forever."

As I say this, a shaft of moonlight falls over the Virgin

Mary's features, and for one second, I believe, truly believe, that there is life after death, that there is magic in the world, that there is a god, and she looks like the thing you love most. I believe my mom can hear me. I believe she is saying, "I love you too." I believe I am not alone.

I pull Mom's necklace from my pocket and clasp it around my neck.

THIRTEEN

That night, I pitch the tent at a campground. It may not be the safest for a woman to sleep alone outside, but I can't bear the thought of being trapped in another crappy motel room. I try to be smart. I set up close to other campers. To my left, a family with several tents and a passel of kids sits at a picnic table playing cards. To my right, an elderly couple prepares for dinner outside their motor home. They have a graying black poodle named Davy Crockett. I know Davy's name because as I'm unzipping the flap to crawl in my tent, he bounds over and humps my leg.

"Davy Crockett!" the woman calls. She stops setting plastic plates on a picnic table long enough to reprimand the offending canine. "Stop molesting that sweet child. Come back here!" Davy runs to her but returns to his object of affection (my ankle) the second she turns her back.

"Davy!" yells the man, who is sitting at the table reading

a book by the light of a lantern. "Get your willy away from that poor girl!"

Normally, Davy would piss me off, but I'm so desperate for a friend, I smile and say, "It's okay!" Crouching, I push him gently away and croon, "Hey, Davy Crockett. How's life?"

When I stand up, Davy returns to his amorous activities.

"I'm so sorry, sweetheart!" The woman stomps over and sweeps the dog into her arms. "Davy, you know better!" She's wearing a men's flannel shirt, probably belonging to her husband. Her short hair is dyed purplish-red. You can tell she used to be pretty. Maybe she still is, and I'm too young to see it. It occurs to me that her husband probably thinks so.

"It's all right," I say. "I get it. I used to have a dog." I had several when Mom was alive, actually. I don't mention that none of them ever carried on an illicit affair with my leg.

"You by yourself?" She looks me up and down, appraising me.

"Yeah," I say.

My answer clearly does not please her. "Have you eaten?"

I can tell she's about to go "protective grandma" on my ass. I consider lying and saying I have eaten, but hunger and loneliness override my antisocial tendencies. "No, I haven't," I say.

"Well, you're having dinner with us," the woman declares. "I'm Jean, by the way." She shifts Davy to one hand and extends the other. I shake it. Her grip is surprisingly strong.

"And I'm Lawrence," the man calls. "That dirty little asshole is Davy Crockett, if you haven't figured that out already."

"Are you sure you don't mind me eating with you?" I ask. It's a silly question, as I'm already following Jean to the picnic table.

"Of course not," she says over her shoulder. "You'll be a welcome change of pace. I get sick of listening to this old bastard drone on and on about airplanes."

"I was in the air force," Lawrence says, beaming as if she paid him a compliment.

We sit at the table, which is spread with a bucket of fried chicken, a container of potato salad, and a basket of biscuits that are probably half butter. Mom would kick my ass if she saw me eating this. Lawrence kisses Jean on the cheek. For a second, I imagine Dean and me like them—old, insulting each other, herding horny poodles at a campground. It warms my heart.

"So what's your name?" Lawrence asks me.

"Oh, I'm sorry. I'm Harley," I say.

"That's an interesting name." Jean plops several drumsticks onto her plate and passes the bucket to me.

I take a breast and wipe my fingers on my jeans. "It's a nickname," I say, pointing to my Harley as if it's explanation enough. "My real name is Juliet."

"I knew a Juliet once," Lawrence says. "Second most gorgeous girl I ever saw."

"Who was the first?" Jean asks.

"Julia Roberts." Lawrence winks. Jean slaps his arm.

We pass around the rest of the food, and then dig in. I hate to say it, but I'm enjoying my foray into unhealthy eating more than I ever dreamed possible. Fried chicken dripping with grease is about a billion times better than baked tofu skewers, for the record.

"So, Juliet," Lawrence says. "What's a pretty girl like you doing out here all alone?"

I consider lying so I won't have to hear someone else say how sorry they are about Mom dying. But with his no-nonsense white buzz cut and still impressive physique, Lawrence looks like the kind of guy who could spot bullshit a mile away. "I'm taking my mom's ashes back home."

Jean's eyes go soft, but she doesn't say she's sorry. "Where's home?"

"New York."

We're quiet for a minute. I watch the moon disappear behind a swath of clouds and emerge again.

"My mom's death nearly did me in," says Jean softly. "She died when I was about your age."

"Yeah?" I say.

"Yeah," says Jean. "Lung cancer. She was really healthy too. Didn't smoke. Didn't drink. None of us saw it coming."

"I'm sorry." It feels good to be the one handing out condolences for once.

"You know, it's been almost forty years, and not a day goes by that I don't miss her." Jean sets another chicken breast on my plate even though I'm not halfway through the first one. "Eat up. There's plenty."

"Thanks," I say, wondering if I have to. I'm not sure I can even finish one.

"How long has it been?" asks Jean.

"Coming up on seven months," I say.

"You must be walking around half dead." Jean places her soft hand over mine for a second then goes back to her dinner.

"Pretty much," I say.

"I know when my mom died, it hurt to think of living my whole life without her," Jean tells me. "She was going to miss all of the important moments. My wedding. My kids being born. I was afraid that by the time I died and saw her again, I'd be someone she wouldn't even recognize."

I nod. I've worried about those things too, even the part about her not knowing me when she saw me again, because for all my grandstanding about not believing in an afterlife, I hope there is one.

"But you know what is strange? Every single time something important happened to me, my mom showed me she was nearby. She loved hummingbirds, and on my wedding day, this hummingbird buzzed my head as I said, 'I do.' When my son was born, a hummingbird showed up on the windowsill at the hospital. Do you know how rare that is, for a hummingbird to sit still like that?"

"No," I say.

"Oh, they never sit still," Lawrence pipes in. "Little bastards are always going, going, going."

Jean smiles. "Lawrence has feeders for his hummers all around our house. Loves them."

"They're beautiful," I agree, deciding not to inform them that the word *hummer* may mean something very different to the younger generation than it does to them.

THE LONG RIDE HOME · 163

"They are indeed," says Jean. "The point is, my mom never really left me. You'll find this out as you move through life. She'll let you know she's around in the oddest ways."

I look down at my chicken. "She already has, I think."

"Of course she has." Jean touches my hand again. "You know, I'm way closer to death now than when my mom left me, and I can tell you that underneath all these wrinkles, I'm still her little girl. Life won't change you as much as you think, at least not the important parts. When you see her again, you'll still be her baby."

"How do you know I'll see her again?" I ask. I expect her to give me some religious diatribe, but she doesn't. Instead, she says, "Close your eyes."

I feel weird, but I do it. A cool breeze brushes my cheeks.

"I have always believed that the truth lives inside you," she says. "I have always followed my heart."

"That's what Mom did too," I say.

"Does your heart say your mom is gone forever?" she asks.

I open my mouth to give her the answer she wants to hear, but I stop. I'm not going to lie to make her feel better. I'm not going to say Mom is still here if she's not. I wait, listening to the wind rustle through the treetops. Behind my closed eyelids, I see Mom's face, smiling. A wave of love washes over me. With it, grief comes too. These things seem to go hand in hand. You pay for love with pain. I'm still not sure it's worth it.

I keep listening. I hear familiar music in the distance. For a second, I can't place it. I focus. It's the band Mom loved,

Roger's band. The song about Jean-Luc Picard. No one but Mom listens to her little indie band from nowhere. And yet, there they are, blaring from the speakers of some motor home a few hundred yards away.

I gasp. The image of Mom remains in my mind's eye, as alive as she was when she was with me. For a second, I'm 100 percent sure Mom is here.

I don't know what happened to her. I don't understand life and death. How could I? I'm a tiny speck of a human on a minuscule dot of a planet in a universe bigger than my ability to comprehend. How could my pea-brain possibly grasp the meaning of existence? Still, when I listen to my heart, it knows a soul as beautiful as hers couldn't just up and vanish.

"She's not gone," I whisper.

"No," Jean says. "And she never will be."

⸺ꞏ⸺

Later, after hours listening to Jean and Lawrence recall their lives' adventures, I return to my tent. They were so kind, I almost forgot to hurt for a while, but as soon as I lie down, the pain comes back, twisting my insides.

After tossing fitfully for an hour, I sleep and dream of Mom and me racing down the freeway on the Harley. She steers. I'm behind her, but somehow, the throttle is mine. I squeeze, harder, harder, harder, watch as the speedometer climbs, fifty, sixty, seventy, eighty. Soon, it's spinning around and around, like a clock hand going way too fast. Somewhere in the distance, the band Mom loved sings about Jean–Luc Picard, and around us, the scenery races past in a blur.

"Harley, slow down!" Mom screams, but I can't.

Our bike lifts off, driving through the sky at warp speed. Stars fly by. Moons. Planets. Galaxies. Mom starts to float away. I clutch at her, but can't hold her. "Don't leave me, Momma!" I cry. She turns to me, waves goodbye, and drifts off into the black nothing of space.

I look down. The motorcycle has become a mangled mass, all twisted steel and smoke. Clinging to the wreckage, I watch Earth fade to a faint blue dot in the distance.

I know I will never go home again.

FOURTEEN

wake up to my phone dinging. I ignore it the first time, but the second time, I roll over. Groaning, I pick it up. It's Dean texting. Harley, call me. I have a right to know if this is my baby.

I shove the phone under my pillow and try to go back to sleep, but I can't. I know I'm being a royal bitch. It's not like I don't feel bad about it. Taking up being a bitch is kinda like taking up smoking. Once you start, it's hard to stop. And it's addictive. Like guilt. You can mainline guilt the way junkies mainline heroin. When it comes right down to it, guilt is my drug of choice. My guilt is the engine that keeps my bitch machine running. I know I should put it down, get clean, and start acting like a sane person again, but it's kinda hard when you're a murderer.

"Honey, you awake in there?" Jean's gentle voice pulls me out of my reverie, if *reverie* is the word you use to describe a particularly intense bout of self-loathing. The sun filters through the mosquito netting at the top of the tent, turning the soft ground into a web of light and shadow.

"Yeah," I say, sitting up and glancing down to make sure my nipples aren't showing through my white T-shirt, should Jean decide to unzip the tent flap and pop her head in. She probably won't, but you never know.

My nipples are showing, and she does.

"Well, aren't we perky?" she says, staring straight at my boobs.

I have no idea how to respond to that.

"I brought you some OJ." She laughs as if she told the best joke, thrusting a Styrofoam cup through the flap. I fumble toward her, trying to cover my chest.

"Oh, sweetheart, don't sweat it. I've seen a breast or two in my day. Believe it or not, mine used to be quite impressive."

I am utterly unsure how to proceed, as we skipped the "protocol for tit conversations with old, purple-haired ladies" section in my manners class. Before I can stop myself, I look at her chest. She too is braless. Far be it from me to impose fashion imperatives on anyone, but I'm gonna go out on a limb and say it's a look she might want to forgo in the future.

She winks. "You could at least pretend not to be horrified."

"What?" I mutter. "I'm not. I mean, I think you look—I wasn't even looking."

"Are those my boobs, or two raccoons wrestling?" she asks gleefully.

My god. Have I been planted in some very unfortunate scene from old people porn?

"They didn't look like this until after the kids," she says. "You want babies?"

I shrug. "I think so. Someday." I do not tell her that she has almost convinced me to return to Planned Parenthood, ASAP.

"Behold your future."

~ల

An hour later, I'm eating cereal at a picnic table with Lawrence and Jean. Jean has put on a bra, thank god. The cereal is some granola shit Mom would have loved. Lawrence is crunching it loudly, and as much as I like him, it makes me want to punch him in the face. There is nothing in the world worse than listening to someone you love chew, except for listening to someone you barely know chew. Chewing is an intimate act. I should not have to think about the inside of anyone else's mouth unless I decide to stick my tongue in it. But dear Lawrence is an aggressive, untidy chewer. He clearly did not have a mother who ordered him to eat with his mouth closed.

"So where you headed next?" he asks.

I barely hear the question through his spoonful of cereal.

I shrug. "Not sure yet. Wherever the wind takes me."

"I like the way you think." Jean extends her plastic spoon in my direction, a queen granting her blessing. "Spread your wings. Enjoy your youth. God knows, it will be gone before you know it."

Who are these depressing old fucks, and what happened to the benevolent angels from last night? I eat what's left of my cereal as quickly as I can without reproducing Lawrence's abominable litany of slurps and chomps. Then I stand, wiping my hands on my jeans.

"Well, thanks for this. It was so awesome meeting both of you. I'd better get going."

"So soon?" Lawrence asks, mercifully setting his spoon down. "We were just getting used to you."

"I'm sorry," I say awkwardly.

"Lawrence," Jean chides, standing. "Don't guilt-trip her. Save that for our own children. They're ours to torture. She isn't."

I laugh.

Jean puts an arm around me and winks meaningfully, as if we have a secret. "She needs to go sow her wild oats."

Holy shit. If I do not get a move on pronto, Jean will surely start sharing the details of her sexual history. "Why, when I was your age, I blew a handsome young man in a subway bathroom," I imagine her saying.

"Okay," I say quickly. "Thanks again." I hug them both. Jean smells like pine, not real pine, but bottled pine.

"You smell nice," I tell her.

"Oh, that's air freshener," she says breezily. "I douse myself with it in the mornings. Quicker than a shower. Cheaper than perfume. You can buy it any convenience store."

I can't help but laugh. "Are you kidding?"

"No," she says, her eyes twinkling playfully. "Why, is that odd?"

"Not at all," I lie.

"You are so full of shit." She smiles. "Lawrence, am I a strange woman?"

"Excessively. And I find it irresistibly sexy," Lawrence says. He puts his arm around her and takes a whiff of her neck. "Mmm. Mountain breeze. My favorite scent."

Jean laughs. "Oh, you pervert."

Davey Crocket must be used to being called "pervert," because he comes running from his place under the table and humps my leg.

"Hey, little dude," I say, trying to extricate my ankle gracefully.

"And so she leaves us just as she found us," Lawrence intones, picking up the writhing canine.

"It's rather poetic, isn't it?" Jean asks wistfully.

As I walk toward my bike, they laugh and call out well wishes.

"Keep in touch," they say.

I pull the business card they gave me out of my pocket. It says *Lawrence and Jean Whittler, Old Farts Extraordinaire* on it. "I've got your info right here."

"We'll miss you," they say in unison.

"I'll miss you too," I yell as I start my Harley.

It's not until I'm racing down the freeway that I realize it's true.

⁓

Had my mom not died, what happened next might have been the defining moment in my life so far. I would measure events as happening "before the wreck" and "after the wreck." But breaking a few bones is nothing compared to losing your only parent, so it wasn't as big of a deal as it could have been.

But I'm rushing ahead. You're confused. I was just saying goodbye to Jean and Lawrence, and now I've wrecked. You need a transition, a rewind. Maybe I should say something like, "It all started when" only I don't know when it all started. How do you decide when a particular episode in your life began? It's not like you have slow fades to indicate scene changes and dramatic music to ease you from one mood to another. Did it start when I was listening to Lawrence slurp his breakfast? When I stopped for gas an hour later? When that asshole flipped me off as I pulled back onto the freeway? Okay, let's go with that last one. That's when it started.

So I had just pulled over at Circle K, filled up the bike, and grabbed a bottle of Gatorade. It was purple, an unfortunate choice as it spilled all over my white shirt when the bike went down, ruining my vintage Bon Jovi tee forever. I guess it didn't really matter though. Even if my drink hadn't spilled, the blood would have ruined my clothes anyway.

Like I said, I'm driving along, my Gatorade lodged in the triangle of seat between my thighs, pissed off for all kinds of reasons, the obvious, constant one being my mother's death. Secondarily, I'm pissed because Dean had the gall to *demand* I call him. I mean, had he asked, it would have been one thing, but demanding is quite another. I'm also furious at the baby in my belly, having finally grasped—I mean really *realized*— that it has put me in a decidedly shitty situation. I can either abort it and feel guilty forever, or I can keep it and end up with boobs like Jean, not to mention a totally screwed-up life. There is a third option, adoption, but that won't fix my tits, now will it? Holy hell. I never wanted to be a stripper, but shouldn't I at least have had the opportunity to consider a life of professional public nudity before the choice was ripped away from me completely? What if I need money for college someday? A *Playboy* centerfold won't even be an option.

So here I am, pissed as all get out, when this dude in a beat-up, gray truck passes me and screams out his window. I can't hear him over the wind, but by the way he's snarling, I deduce that he's not trying to let me know my rear tire is low. And then, lest I miss his point, he flips me off. That does it. I snap.

"You douchebag!" I scream, and I squeeze the throttle hard.

People have not evolved much beyond their reptilian brain stems. Don't let anyone tell you different. They have survival instincts that kick in when they are truly threatened, gut feelings that override all logic and make them get the hell out of Dodge when a maniac is chasing them down the freeway on a Harley, screaming epithets, even if the maniac in question is a girl who might weigh 125 pounds if her pockets were full of rocks. This guy is huge—his neck is bigger than my thigh—but he must get that I'm not quite sane because instead of engaging in a battle of words, he guns it.

"Where are you going, chickenshit?" I shriek, staring at

the back of his shaved head glinting through his rear windshield. My blood pounds in my temples, making a drum of my helmet. My hands clench. I'm crying again. Why I am crying now, of all times? All this asshat needs is to see my weakness.

Instantly, he becomes everything I hate in the world. He's my mom, who died on me without warning. He's Dean, who had the audacity to get me pregnant and now wants answers. He's the baby inside me, who insists I make a life-defining decision I'm not even moderately equipped to make. The douchebag is fleeing, but I'm gaining on him. Yellow lines fly along beneath me, a thousand bright warbirds accompanying me as I attack. I'm getting closer. I can make out the nipples on the silver naked ladies on his mud flaps, which makes me hate him even more. "Chauvinist pig!"

And then, he slows down. I don't know why. Maybe a dog runs across the highway. That's what he claims later when the police ask, but whatever the reason, I see brake lights. I brake slowly, like I should, fast enough not to plaster myself all over his bumper, but slowly enough that the wheels don't lock up. I feel this weird satisfaction, knowing I'm pulling this off, maneuvering myself through a dangerous situation. I'm veering onto the shoulder, still slowing steadily, when this stump materializes from out of nowhere. It's suddenly there. I do what I shouldn't. I brake fast, locking the wheels, and I'm skidding, going down, trying to remember what Mom taught me. "Let go of the bike," I hear her say. Maybe it's inside my head, maybe out loud. I listen and let go, but not fast enough, because something snaps, and pain shoots through my arm.

People say this shit happens in slow motion, but it doesn't. One second, my tires lock up and I think, "Shit!" The next, my head smacks something hard, like taking a sledgehammer to my skull, and the next, I wake up in a hospital.

FIFTEEN

lied. Waking up in the hospital wasn't the next thing that happened. I was going to leave this part out, but it doesn't seem honest, and if I'm going to bother to write this at all, I want you to know who I really am, even if that is crazy.

So the next thing that happened was I saw my mom. To this day, it still makes me cry to think of it. As I was going down, there was this weird shrieking in my ears. It was the loudest sound I'd ever heard. Some of it was the tires skidding, but mostly, I think it was death closing in. And then, everything was quiet. Dead quiet. A quiet I've never known before or since.

I would like to say that I found myself standing in front of some pearly gates or hovering above my body, but that's not how it was. I wasn't anywhere. I was simply floating in indescribable…what? Light. That's the only word I know to describe it, but it wasn't the insubstantial stuff that comes out of chandeliers. This light was thick. This light had substance. Forgive my cheesy-as-fuck-ness, but this light was liquid love. I wasn't scared anymore, not even a little bit.

"Mom?" I called. Yeah, I could talk. Even though I didn't have a body. Even though I didn't have a mouth. I could think and make noise even though I didn't have a head. "Mom," I said again. Somehow I knew she was there.

She kinda faded into the scene, grew out of the light like one of those flowers blossoming from seed in fast motion on nature shows. She was perfect, wearing her leather jacket, as I remembered her, only with that amazing light seeping from her pores.

"Hi, my baby," she said, the same words she said to me the first time she held me. She kissed me on the face, even though I didn't have a face. That's just what it was. I had no body. She had one. And she could kiss me.

"'But soft,'" she said. "'What light from yonder window breaks?'" She looked at me in a way no one before or since has ever looked at me, the way only a mom can look at her little girl, like I was the Taj Mahal and pyramids and Niagara Falls all rolled into one "'It is the east, and Juliet is the sun.'"

"Mom, am I dead?" I asked.

She smiled a secret smile, the way she used to the night before Christmas when I begged to know what my presents were. "Oh, monkey," she said gently. "We never die."

And that's when I woke up.

~e~

Have you ever imagined what it might feel like to be peeled with a vegetable peeler? I have because I'm twisted like that. If you are too, then you can sort of picture what I felt when I woke. Mom's now-tattered jacket had protected my arms, but the asphalt ate through the skin on my right hand, leaving it raw and bloody. My arm got tangled with the bike and was broken in two places. A rookie mistake. Mom would have kicked my ass if she saw.

The worst part was what happened to my head. Later, when I saw my helmet, Mom's name was shattered, a web of blunt trauma, as if it had taken most of the impact. I didn't know that when I woke up though. If this was what happened with a helmet, I'd hate to see what it would have been like without a helmet. My skull felt like Godzilla was tap-dancing on it. And joy to the world, my collarbone was also broken. It wasn't pretty; I was feeling the hurt.

So rewind with me to the moment I wake up. All I know is I wished I hadn't. I've never felt pain like this. Not even close.

"Where am I?" I shriek, which is cliché of me, a line Mom and I would have dropped into the mouth of an invalid from our soap operas. Cut me some slack though. Five seconds ago, I was floating in liquid light with my dead mother.

"You're in the hospital," a woman's gentle voice says.

"Mom?"

"No, sweetie."

I open my eyes, or at least I try. They feel sort of stuck shut. "I can't see," I say, panicking.

"Your face is swollen," the voice says. I finally open my eyes far enough to see that the voice belongs to a woman with a blond pixie cut. She's wearing pink scrubs. "Don't worry. Your eyes are fine. Your face is too. Or it will be."

She adds that last part like she thinks I'm worried about what I look like. I'm not. I'm not coherent enough for that. Still, I'm aware enough to know I might appreciate the information later on when I look in a mirror.

Gently, the nurse sweeps my hair from my face. For a second, she reminds me of Mom. "I hope you don't mind, but we went through your phone to call your next of kin. Your mom didn't answer."

"She can't. She's dead."

The nurse looks sad.

Don't. Say. It.

She says it. "I'm sorry."

I try to wave away her condolences, but it hurts my shoulder. "Shit!" I say through clenched teeth.

"You shouldn't move. You're due for more pain meds. I'll get you some." The nurse goes through a laundry list of my injuries. I try to take it in, but my mind is reeling.

"How long have I been here?" I ask when she stops to take a breath.

"Two days," she answers. "You were in a coma."

"A coma?"

"Yes," she says. "Brains are fragile. Yours took quite a blow."

"Stupid stump," I say.

"Stump?"

"Never mind." I try to shake my head. It feels like Mike Tyson punches my face. "Fuck," I say, gasping.

"Try to stay still," the nurse says. "I'll get those meds." She stands. "Dean will be here soon."

I jump at his name, in spite of her admonitions. "Fuck!" I say again. "Dean?"

"Since we couldn't get ahold of your mom, we called the next person in your 'favorites' list. Dean was very worried about you. He's on his way."

SIXTEEN

When I was little, Mom used to talk about warp speed every time we'd drive through a snowstorm. The flakes would be coming at the windshield, looking like planets and stars flying by a spaceship, and she'd say, "Get ready, honey. We're going into warp speed." She'd push the magic button, which I now know was the hazard lights, and the warp triangle would flash red on the control panel. Squealing with glee, we'd fly along like that, two space travelers traversing a dark universe.

Now I'm wondering if Mom pushed the warp speed button on my life. Was there a control panel in that white light? I didn't think to look. But everything is happening way too fast. Everywhere I turn, asteroids and planets and meteors rush at me. It's anything but gleeful.

The most recent bit of space debris to show up in my orbit is wearing an Edgar Allan Typoe T-shirt when he walks into my hospital room. It features a very forlorn-looking Edgar Allan receiving a rejection letter for his story "The Ramen." It's funny, so I laugh, which makes my head hurt, which makes me cry.

Deans lopes to me and kisses my forehead. "You scared me," he says. He's trying not to cry, which makes me cry harder. He sits on the bed. I wince. "I'm sorry," he says. "Does that hurt you? Should I stand?" He starts to get up.

"No, don't get up. Please. Stay with me." I clutch at him like I clutched at the Asshole right after I lost my virginity, which makes me feel vulnerable and shitty, but what are you gonna do? No way am I going to pull off my "I am a rock" routine, what with the bandages and the IV and my face looking like Gordon Ramsay went at it with a cheese grater. I keep clutching.

Dean takes my hand and presses it to his lips. They're warm and soft. They feel like home. "You're a pain in my ass, but I love you," he says.

I laugh through my tears, tasting snot. "I love you too, Typoe Boy."

For a second, he seems like he's going to address the fact that I just said "I love you" for the first time, but he doesn't. Instead, he says, "Typoe Boy?"

I glance at his shirt.

He looks down and flattens the shirt so I can see the picture better. "Oh, yeah. I forgot I was wearing this. You get why it's funny, right?"

"Yeah, dork. I get it. I took freshman English."

"Just making sure. I didn't know if you were still concussing or whatever."

"I'm definitely still whatevering."

He kisses my hand once more. "If you ever almost die on me again, I'll kick your ass."

"I think I'm done with near-death experiences," I say.

Dean glances around the room, taking in the institutional decor and the various implements of torture. He touches the giant bouquet of sunflowers that sits on my nightstand. "Mercy?" he asks.

"Yeah," I say. "She's coming tonight. They called you instead of her, so she didn't know."

"Oh, shit! I totally should have called her," he says. "I'm sorry. I thought for sure she knew, and I just wanted to get to you. I drove ninety all the way."

"Apparently, the nurses decided you were the second-most important person in my life."

Dean laughs.

I touch one of his curls, loving the way it falls along his jawline. "I'm not sure they were right."

He nods. "I know. This must be weird for you."

I shake my head. "You aren't the second-most important person. You're the first."

He squints at me, seemingly trying to decide whether I'm telling the truth or high on pain meds. "You mean that, Harley? Because I can't go three seconds without thinking about you. I swear to Jesus, the idea of living my life without you scares the shit out of me."

"You don't even believe in Jesus."

"Yes, I do." He pulls a crucifix from under his shirt. "You didn't notice this while you were licking my chest?"

I feel myself blush. "I saw that, but I thought you meant it ironically."

"No irony whatsoever. I gave up on church a long time ago, but I never gave up on the Dude."

I almost start quoting *The Big Lebowski*, but I'm not sure he'll get the movie reference, and anyway, it might offend him. So I say, "Oh, well, you never told me that."

"You never asked."

"I guess I never asked a lot of things about you."

He smiles. "You were too busy busting my balls to ask questions."

I smile back. "In addition to being done with near-death experiences, I'm also thinking of cutting back on ball busting."

"So ask me a question."

I think of questions I could ask. What's your favorite color? What's your best memory from second grade? But I ask the one I really want an answer to. "Why do you love me? I'm such a bitch."

"No, you're not," says Dean. "You're hurt, and you're scared, and you're always posturing, but you're not a bitch. You have a beautiful heart and a great mind. I never believed your bitch routine for a second."

"Posturing?" I repeat, feeling mildly insulted. "I'm so not posturing."

"You definitely are," he says. "You're like one of

those apes in the zoo pounding your chest to scare away potential attackers."

I laugh.

"But, Harley, let's get one thing straight, okay?"

"Okay," I say.

"I'm not an attacker. We're on the same team."

Nodding, I touch his arm.

"My turn to ask a question," he says.

I know what it's going to be before he says it, but he asks anyway. "The baby *is* mine, right?"

I nod. "There was never anyone but you." Then I realize I'm sick and tired of lying. "Okay, there was, but he was in New York before I even met you. I was just being a bitch that day in the hotel." Dean looks uber-relieved, like he'd believed he had cancer only to learn the tests were all wrong. I feel sick at the thought of how much I must have hurt him. I say the words I've never said to anyone I've wronged before. "I'm sorry."

He shakes his head. "It's all right. I'm glad you're okay. And the baby. I mean, it is okay, right?"

I smile, which surprises me. I wasn't expecting to be happy about this. "Yeah," I say. "Amazingly, she's still in there, doing fine."

His face lights up. "She?"

"They did an ultrasound to make sure she was okay. I saw her heart beating. The doctor said it may be too early to tell, but he was pretty sure it's a girl."

"Oh my fucking god." Dean starts to cry.

We clutch at each other and sob for a long, long time. We are idiots, sitting broken under florescent lights, smelling bleach, weeping for happiness about a baby we can't possibly raise. We aren't old enough. We aren't wise enough. We aren't established enough. But we cry because we know that sometimes, miracles grow from the most unlikely soil. Sometimes, roses bloom in the desert.

SEVENTEEN

'm peeing when Mercy shows up. The bathroom door is
closed, but I can hear her through the wall.

"Dean!" She says his name in that desperate, dramatic
way people use to address one another in hospital rooms.
"Where is she?" As if I have been whisked away to brain
surgery or abducted by aliens.

"In the bathroom," Dean says.

"I'm in here," I call, wanting to reassure her. I've already
put the poor woman through enough shit without adding
possible anal probing by aliens to her list of worries. "I'll be
there in a second." The nurse, whose name turned out to
be Anastasia, has given me my pain meds,which the doctor
says won't hurt the baby as long as I only take them for a
little while. She's rockin' for a fifty-year-old lady. She rides a
Harley on the weekends, and she knows exactly how to put
in an IV needle without making a girl hurt. Sometimes, she

spends her breaks in my room, talking about life. Her name isn't actually Anastasia—she changed it when she joined a cult. She left the cult years ago, but the moniker stuck.

My meds are kicking in, so I feel almost numb. I struggle to get toilet paper from the roll and wipe. Everything is harder when one arm is in a cast, and the other is hooked up to a roll-along IV unit. As I fumble at the paper with my good hand, my ineptitude makes me giggle.

Mercy knocks. "Are you okay in there, honey?"

"Not at all." I gasp. "I can't even wipe."

"Are you crying?"

"No, I'm laughing."

"Can I open the door?" It sounds like she's smiling, probably with relief. "I'll help."

If I weren't on drugs, the prospect of Mercy helping me wipe might be humiliating. As is, it's hilarious. "The door's unlocked," I say through peals of laughter.

The door swings open, and there she is, ready and willing to wipe my ass in her tiger-striped, movie star sunglasses and rainbow-colored maxi dress. It's probably the drugs that make me burst into tears. That, and it just feels so damn good to see her.

"Oh, kid," she says, rushing to me. "It's no big deal. I'll help." She reaches for the toilet paper, but I stop her by throwing my good arm around her neck. My IV line gets caught in her hair.

She hugs me back, squeezing tightly enough that it hurts even through the meds. "Ow, ow, ow!" I say.

"Sorry!" she says, backing off. She's crying too. Mercy never cries.

"Why are you crying?" I ask.

"Because you're an idiot, and I love you," she says. She raises her fist to punch me in the arm and then seems to realize that's a bad idea. "If you ever do something that stupid again, I swear, I'll punch you, cast or no cast."

Why do people keep threatening to hurt me because I got hurt? "It's not like I wrecked on purpose," I say.

"I know." She hugs me again, gently this time. "I know." Then she wipes her eyes and yanks some toilet paper from the roll. "Should I..." She holds the wad in front of her awkwardly, as if she doesn't know what to do with it.

"No freaking way. I'm not that high." I take it from her and wipe as best I can. It's ineffectual, but that's better than a thorough wiping courtesy of Mercy. When I'm done, I try to stand, but I can't get any leverage, what with the whole broken arm thing. "Give me a hand?" I ask.

Mercy does. As we walk back to my bed, she puts an arm around my waist for support, which doesn't really help, but I don't say so. I want her to feel like she's being useful. Dean's sitting in a lime-green chair next to my bed. He hasn't moved since he got here.

"She's alive," Mercy says.

He grins. Those teeth. My heart pounds. "Thank god," he says.

I sink slowly onto the mattress and awkwardly adjust my

body. "Did you know Dean actually believes in god?" I use the mechanical controls to bring the bed to a sitting position.

"I didn't," Mercy says, pulling the other lime-green chair next to Dean. She sits.

I lean back on my pillow. "His unbroken tattoo is about the way he felt after he found Jesus. It was after a skiing accident. He broke both legs."

"Who woulda thunk?" Mercy asks.

"Not me," I say. "I never knew. Also, it turns out he likes rats. A lot. When he was a kid, he had three of them as pets, but it broke his heart when they died, so he never got more. Their names were John, Ringo, and Paul."

"No love for George?" Mercy yanks the blanket up over my legs even though it's about a bazillion degrees. Again, I let her because I want her to feel useful.

Dean strokes my leg. Since he got here, he hasn't stopped touching me. "I tried for a George. My mom said three rats were more than enough."

"She clearly didn't understand the significance of the Fab Four," Mercy says sympathetically. "Fab Three doesn't have the same ring."

Dean laughs. "In her defense, we already had a golden retriever, two cats, and a snake, all of whom she was forced to take care of because I always forgot."

"Dean is very scatterbrained." I offer another of the Dean tidbits I've gleaned during the hours we've spent together in this room. "He once put his keys in the fridge and couldn't find them for days."

Mercy chuckles. "Sounds like me."

It does sound like Mercy. Once, I called her from school and asked her to bring me lunch, and she brought me her laptop. To this day, I have no idea what she was thinking. I didn't ask because I didn't want to hurt her feelings.

"So you get out of here tomorrow, huh?" Mercy asks.

"Yeah," I say. "I'm busting out of this joint."

"Good! I cleared out the back seat and put some pillows back there. You can ride home in style."

Home? It had not occurred to me that I might be going back to LA instead of finishing my journey. Going back feels all wrong. I remember Mom telling me to follow my heart. "I wasn't planning on going home," I say. "I don't think I'm finished."

Mercy tries not to look worried. "Well, you certainly can't go riding across the country on a motorcycle with your injuries. And we don't even know if the motorcycle's rideable."

"It isn't," I say. "I talked to the garage where it was towed. It will be a few weeks before it's ready. But I was thinking maybe Dean could drive me?" I look at him imploringly. "I mean, if he thinks he can put up with my shit for a little longer."

Dean beams like he won an Olympic gold medal. "Hells to the yeah," he says.

Mercy touches his arm gratefully. "Okay, I guess." She takes off her sunglasses. When she smiles, the exquisite skeins of wrinkles around her eyes deepen. "As long as Dean is with you."

Something happens to me then. I look at these two

people who obviously give tons of shits about me, who would do anything to make sure I was protected, happy, and loved, and bliss washes over me. It's almost like I'm back in the light with Mom. It's a this-world version of heaven. I feel safe. I feel cherished. Even though I burned my house to the ground, I feel like I'm almost home.

~ᘓ

The next day, they release me from the hospital with a prescription for pain meds and a long list of things I should and shouldn't do while I'm recovering. Anastasia seems sad when I say goodbye. "You're an amazing woman," she says as she pushes me out to the parking lot in a wheelchair. For some reason, I'm not allowed to walk. "You're strong. Take care of you."

Mercy walks beside Anastasia, holding one of the handles. Anastasia lets her help, just like I do when Mercy wants to feel useful. Next to me, Dean carries my saddlebag. Miraculously, Mom's ashes survived, though the urn did not. I think shattering the shit out of her container was her final commentary on having been neglected on a counter next to the Oreos for so long. But the saddlebag didn't tear, so Mom's ashes are in there at the bottom, mixed up with ceramic shards and T-shirts.

I smile at Anastasia. "I've never really thought of myself as strong," I say.

"I think you're wrong about that," she says. She helps me into Dean's beat-up blue truck. It's vintage, he likes to say, which means it's a piece of shit.

"Are you comfortable?" Anastasia asks, kindly. She's good at making people feel loved, which I guess goes with the job description, but there's something about her. She's not only doing a job. She actually cares. This morning, she brushed my hair and helped me into a pair of jeans and one of Dean's giant T-shirts before he and Mercy arrived. As I say goodbye, I'm surprised how emotional I feel. She makes me consider the possibility that people aren't all heartless assholes. I watch her walk away, her pixie cut gleaming in the sun.

Mercy puts on my seat belt, and even though it makes me feel like an invalid, I let her because, well, you know.

"Be safe," she says, kissing me on the forehead. Mom used to say that emphatically when I walked out the door, as if her words had the power to conjure mysterious protective forces. I wonder if she would still be here if I had said those same words to her as she left my bedroom the night of the fire. "Anastasia was right." Mercy looks into my eyes. "You *are* strong. You're one of my heroes, kid."

"You're one of mine." I hug her hard with my good arm. "I'll miss you."

Mercy starts to head toward her car, and then I remember the necklace I bought for her in Omaha. "Wait!" I say. "I have something for you."

She returns, and I ask Dean to open the saddlebag and find the necklace. He digs around. When he pulls it out, it's covered in ashes. I hand it to Mercy. "This is for you. I bought it at the store where Mom got me this." I lift my sun necklace.

Mercy's eyes get wet. "Thank you," she says, studying the turquoise moon.

"I'd put it on you, but…" I look at my broken arm.

She laughs. "I'm perfectly capable of putting it on myself. It's one of the most beautiful gifts I've ever been given."

"I just wanted you to know I love you," I say. "I'm lucky to have you."

We say goodbye one last time. I take her in, memorizing her, in case this is the last time I see her. "I love you!" I call out the window again as we turn onto the street, wanting to make double sure I don't make the same mistake I made with Mom. Smiling, she waves.

"Let's get this party started," Dean says as we pull onto the highway. He turns the radio up, and Bob Dylan sings Mom's song about the highway of diamonds. It's getting harder and harder to believe she isn't still with me. I remember what she said to me in that white light. "Oh, monkey, we never die." I feel a vaguely familiar splash inside me, like an almost-forgotten ocean breaking against my rib cage. I think it's hope.

I stare out the window, watching trees and billboards sprint past, pondering how Anastasia and Mercy said I was strong. It occurs to me that I have survived something most people would not. Mom used to spout inspirational clichés like she was a walking Instagram meme, and one of them was, "What doesn't kill you can only make you stronger." I normally rolled my eyes when she said it, as she usually did so when I was whining about doing the dishes or carrying groceries, but now, it feels profound and true. All this shit I've been through has changed me, and maybe, just maybe, it's for the better. Yeah, I'm beat up. Yeah, I look like shit. But under all the pain, I've found a strength, a metal at my core I didn't know was there until now.

For at least a good three minutes, the drive is all birds swooping in front of the truck and sunrays bursting through clouds. I'm exhilarated. Keep in mind that may be the drugs talking. I can see why people get hooked on pain meds. As I start to think my newfound contentment is a permanent condition, Dean goes and bursts my bubble. "So where are we going?"

Even through the meds, I feel fear. I have no idea where we're going. New York is the short answer. But driving straight there doesn't seem right. For one thing, I'm not quite ready to say goodbye to Mom's ashes. For another, I still don't know what to do with this baby. I'm pretty sure I've decided abortion isn't for me, but I still can't imagine raising a kid. Nor can I imagine letting one go. The thought of putting my precious not-so-maybe-baby girl into someone else's arms makes my stomach clench. I have no clue what to do. The road is, always has been, the only place the world makes sense to me. This is more than a road trip. It's a quest, a pilgrimage. Intuitively, I know Mom's highway of diamonds has more to teach me. Leaning my head against the cool window, I ponder Dean's question and squeeze my eyes shut. *Mom,* I think, *where should I go?*

I'm not saying she answers me. Maybe it's my brain. Or my soul. Maybe the best, smartest part of me rises to the surface and gives me the answer. But before I really process what I'm saying, I blurt out, "I need to find my dad."

EIGHTEEN

When I run a Google search for Andy Warphol, my iPhone helpfully asks, "Did you mean Andy Warhol?" and offers a bunch of pictures of soup in answer to my query.

"No, you dumb ass," I say out loud.

"What did I do now?" Dean asks. His crappy truck doesn't have air-conditioning, so he has his window rolled down and his elbow out the window. The wind rustles his hair, making him look like he's at a photo shoot for Axe for Men, which is to say, he's dead shmexy. I remember how good it felt to have him inside me. And I want him. I wonder if my arm would rebreak if I tried to have sex with him in the truck. I'm guessing it would, plus we might get arrested, and I've had more than enough catastrophes for one road trip, thank you very much. Also, for reasons I can't fully understand, the thought of having sex with him terrifies me, as tempting as it is. I'm not sure I'm ready to be that close to him again. What if I freak out like I did last time? So when I answer, I don't hint at my surging lust. Instead, I say, "I'm not talking to you. I'm talking to my phone."

"What did *it* do now?" he asks.

"It thinks I'm running a search for Andy Warhol instead of my dad." I shift in my seat, peeling away from the sticky upholstery.

"Why the hell would it think that?"

"Because my dad's name is Andy Warphol."

Dean laughs, then quiets. "You're not kidding?"

"No," I say. "At least that's what my mom told me his name was. Maybe she made it up. I don't know."

"So if your mom had stayed with your dad, you'd be Harley Warphol? It sounds like a comic book heroine."

"Juliet Warphol, actually," I say.

"Wait. What?"

"My real name is Juliet. Harley's a nickname."

"Holy shit. How did I fall in love with you without knowing your name?" Dean asks.

I shrug apologetically. "I was doing my best to be a walking conundrum."

He grins. "Juliet. I like it."

"I don't," I say. "Hence the nickname. Don't you dare think about calling me Juliet."

"Fair enough." He touches my face. "Harley it is."

I grab his fingers and kiss them, then run a search for "Andy Warphol address."

"Are you looking for Andy Warhol address?" my phone asks.

"No, dumb ass!" I say.

"You and your phone have quite a tense relationship," Dean offers.

"If I didn't need it, I'd throw it out the window," I agree, clicking on "search instead for Andy Warphol's address." This time, one address comes up, an art studio in Minneapolis called Warphol Dreams, which sounds like the name of a kick-ass band, a B sci-fi movie, or a bad porno. I can't decide which.

My stomach lurches. "I think I found him."

Dean glances at me. "No shit?" He rests his hand reassuringly on my thigh, and his heat floods me. Even in the sticky summer air, it feels good.

"You sure you're ready for this?" Dean asks.

I'm not sure, but I nod anyway. "I need to know."

Dean doesn't ask for specifics, which is good, because I'm not sure I have an immediate answer for him. Do I need to know what my dad looks like? Do I need to know if he loved my mom? Or do I need to know if he loved me? Tears come to my eyes when I think that last question. So that must be the right answer.

"I think I need to know if he loved me," I whisper.

"He had to love you," Dean says.

"Why?" I ask.

"Because to know you is to love you."

I smile. "He didn't know me."

"But I bet he felt you, the way I feel this little one." He touches my belly affectionately. "I feel her spirit, you know?"

I nod. I do know.

He points at the sun, which glows white-yellow, almost at its highest point in the sky. "You're like that."

"Like what?"

He smiles. "'Juliet is the sun.'"

Predictably, I burst into tears.

⁓

It takes me three hours, a box of fries, and two cheeseburgers to get over the fact that Dean said my mom's line to me. Sure, it's pretty well-known Shakespeare, right up there with, "To be, or not to be? That is the question." Still, it feels like more than a coincidence.

After I recover from the shock of Dean quoting my mom quoting Shakespeare, it takes me a chocolate shake and another half hour to work up the courage to call the studio. I'll save you the horror of watching me eat twice my weight in junk food. There are copious quantities of ketchup involved and several unseemly belches. Let's fast-forward to when I'm finally feeling brave.

Dean and I are sitting at a rest stop haloed by horizons the color of peace, which is to say, the palest, most perfect blue. As I dial, the serene sky mocks me, standing in stark contrast to the terror riding the waves of my circulatory system. My blood pounds. I can barely breathe. The trash left over from our gluttony-fest is wadded up on the picnic table in front of us. Holding the phone to my ear with my shoulder, I poke at a leftover french fry, waiting for the call to connect.

Dean tosses a crust to the gaggle of pigeons that have gathered since we sat down. Apparently, Dean's really into feeding birds. Consequently, he's an avian rock star. They're his groupies, hanging on his every move. Their iridescent feathers glint in the sun as they flap their wings, bobbing and pecking at the bread. The phone starts to ring. I hang up.

"No answer?" Dean asks.

I shake my head. "I can't go through with it."

"Yes, you can," Dean says. "You can totally do this."

"What are you? A life coach?" I ask. "You should get your own TED Talk."

"I know you," Dean says. "You're the strongest person I've ever seen."

Why do people keep saying that? Maybe because it works. Momentarily, it's like my spine is made of granite. I am woman, hear me roar, and all that shit. Who knew I could be so easily motivated by pep talks? Again, I dial, and this time, I don't hang up. A woman answers. "Warphol Dreams," she says.

"Um, hi," I say.

Beaming, Dean nods encouragingly, as if I have given a particularly moving Oscar acceptance speech.

"Hello," the woman says politely.

"Is this Warhpol Dreams Studio?" I ask, feeling like an idiot. She already told me that. I want to bludgeon myself in the face with my phone and say, "Stupid, stupid, stupid!"

She pauses. "Yes, it is."

"Is Andy Warphol there?"

Dean nods again, squeezing my knee. He's so easily impressed.

"Can I tell him who's calling?" the woman asks.

"Sure. Um, an old friend of…his family," I say.

"Can I give him your name?" The woman asks this suspiciously, as if she's not sure of my intentions. She must think I'm a salesperson or a con artist. Or maybe a prank caller. Do people still do that? Call and ask if the toilet is running, and then tell the unsuspecting victim to go catch it? I've seen it in movies, but I've never tried it myself. I guess that particular brand of petty cruelty probably went out of fashion when caller IDs became commonplace, but even in this day and age, a guy named Andy Warphol has to get his fair share of prank calls.

"I'm Harley," I say. "I think he knew my mom."

"One moment please." The woman still sounds unconvinced, but she leaves to get him.

"Oh, shit. He's coming," I whisper. I almost hang up again, but Dean looks so elated, I can't bear to disappoint him.

"This is Andy Warphol." My heart leaps at the sound of his voice. It's deep, pleasant, and comforting. I don't know what I expected. Some depressed, washed-up drug addict in a trailer park, I guess.

"Hello," I say.

"Hi," he says. "How can I help you?"

"This is kinda awkward," I say, "but did you know a Mary Young?"

He doesn't answer for a long time. For a moment, I think he's going to hang up. Finally, he says "yes" hesitantly. I strongly suspect the memories I'm dredging up are either really good—too good—or really bad. I look at Dean. He nods again and smiles.

Breathing deeply, I say, "Well, she was my mom, and she told me you're my dad."

For a moment, the call breaks up, and all I hear is garbled speech and static, as if my phone signal has been impacted by dropping a bomb on poor, unsuspecting Andy Warphol. So I don't hear what he says in reply to my announcement. But he says something.

"What did you say?" I ask.

And he says, "She went ahead and had you?"

My stomach drops. "What?"

"I'm sorry," he says. "I'm not thinking clearly. This is all so…shit."

"Yeah, it is." I pick a fry off the table and toss it to the pigeons. They go mad with joy. It feels good to be creating happiness. I bounce my leg up and down so hard, it might fall off. Dean puts his arm around my waist. I smell the salty sweetness of him, and my leg slows.

"What's your name?" Andy Warphol asks.

"Harley," I say.

"She named you after her motorcycle?"

"Well, no. I picked the nickname when I was in middle school. I hated my real name."

"What's your real name?"

"Juliet."

There is a sound on the other end of the line. It takes me a minute to realize that Andy Warphol is crying. "She gave you the name I picked for you," he says. "When we first found out about you, I touched her belly and said, 'It is the east, and Juliet is the sun.'"

My chest starts to hurt. A panic attack is coming on. "Wait," I say. "I thought Mom picked my name."

Andy Warphol must not know what to say because he doesn't say anything.

I push for an answer. "You picked my name?"

"We both did," he says. "When we met, Mary—your mom—was playing Juliet in the UCLA production of *Romeo and Juliet*. I was painting the sets. But, yeah. I was the one who said it first."

I'm dizzy. On one hand, it sounds a hell of a lot like my dad loved me. On the other hand, it sounds a hell of a lot like my mom has been lying to me all my life. When no Mexican soap operas were playing, she and I used to watch reruns of *I Love Lucy* together. We'd laugh at Desi when he told Lucy she had some 'splainin' to do. Mom would too, only she's not here to do it.

I breathe deeply, the way I'm supposed to when I'm having a panic attack. It works, probably because the pain meds are muting my emotions. Thank god. My mom isn't around anymore, but my dad is, so I ask, "Would you mind if I came to see you?"

And he says, "I would love that."

Which is how that evening, I end up in Minneapolis.

The city is deep green and moist. The air smells like rain. I take my pain meds a half hour before we arrive at the studio so I won't freak out. When we get there, a woman gives us peach tea—I don't know what's in that shit, but it's good—and then, she goes in back to fetch Andy Warphol. Or my dad. I'm not sure what to call him.

"This is so cool," Dean says, staring at a wall full of Andy's art. He's right. The paintings are mind-bending. Think Salvador Dalí meets *The Walking Dead*. Lots of weird, warped, zombie-looking creatures inhabiting otherworldly dreams- capes that are somehow disturbing and beautiful all at once.

Dean and I are staring at this picture of an emaciated woman, half skeleton, half human, tenderly holding a crying baby to her breast, when I hear a voice behind me. His voice. I've only heard it once, but I know it. It must be biology or something. "Hi, Juliet," he says shyly.

I turn. He's tall, like me. I notice that first. He hasn't shaved in a few days, and his beard is mostly gray. He's handsome though, angular and kind-looking, wearing a flannel shirt. His eyes are the same dark brown as mine. I immediately want to hug him. Which is weird. I don't do it. Instead I say, "Hi." Dean takes my hand.

"You're as pretty as your mom," he says, tearing up.

I revert to form and try to deflect emotional depth with humor. "Now I know where I got my propensity for crying in public." It doesn't work. I tear up too. I always tried to tell myself I didn't care that I didn't have a dad, but now, looking at him, I understand how much I wished I had one.

He laughs. "Yeah, I'm a wimp. Bad asses don't become painters."

"I like your work," I say.

"Thanks." He points to the one Dean and I were looking at. "That one is about your mom. I never really got over her. Or you."

I don't know what to say to that. If he never got over me, where the hell was he? I'm not sure I'm brave enough to ask him. Dean is.

"Why didn't you see her then?" he asks, pulling me closer to him. Did I mention I love Dean?

Taking a deep breath, Andy shuffles his feet and puts his hands in his jean pockets. "Look, I'm not sure what your mom told you, but I didn't even know you existed until you called. I mean, I knew she was pregnant, but the last I heard, she was going to…"

I stare at him. He doesn't say it, but I know what he means. She was going to abort me. The one time I should cry, I don't. I can only stare. "No, she wasn't," I say, getting mad. Who is this asshole anyway? How dare he talk about Mom like this? "She loved me from the moment I was inside her." I know the story of my birth the way preachers know verses from the Bible.

He takes a step forward, reaching for me. I step back.

"I'm not trying to hurt you," he says. "Your mom was an awesome woman. She *did* love you, but she was scared. You can't imagine how terrifying it all was."

I can't?

"Fuck you," I say.

"Please, Juliet. If I had known you were out there, I would have given anything to be in your life. I knew I wanted you. Your mom wasn't sure. She didn't think we had what it took to be parents. And then, there was that fight. I don't even remember what it was over anymore. Soap, I think. I didn't like the brand of soap she bought. I was an asshole back then. An asshole and an alcoholic. I've been sober for eighteen years. That day changed me."

I want to run, get the hell out of here and never look back. Instead, I ask, "What happened?"

"I fucked up. I hit her. She packed up her stuff and left. I mean, of course she did. She should have. She said she was getting an abortion. Those were the last words she said to me. 'I'm getting an abortion.' I never heard from her again." He looks at me beseechingly, silently begging me to forgive him. Suddenly, I hate that my eyes look like his.

I imagine Mom taking this loser's fist to her face, and I want to kill him. I see her running off alone, a little older than I am, trying to come to terms with all the shit I've been trying to come to terms with. I look at Dean, standing beside me, breathing hard like he's mad too, and I know how lucky I am. No matter what I choose, Dean will stay with me. He told me that. I'm not alone. And he would never hurt me. I can't say I forgive Mom for wanting to abort me. I haven't even had time to absorb what this douchebag is saying. But the one thing I do understand is that he punched my mom.

"Please, Juliet," he says. "Don't hate me. I've missed you all my life, the dream of you. And your mom? Man, Mary was the great love of my life."

And finally, finally, I have it, the weapon I need to hurt this piece of shit as badly as he just hurt me. "Yeah?" I say. "Well, the great love of your life died screaming."

I turn around and run.

~e

We stay at a nice hotel that night. Screw money. I need something pretty. The room is gorgeous. Impressionist landscapes hang on the walls, and a picture window overlooks the sleeping city. I stand by it for hours, watching colored lights twinkle below me and white lights twinkle above, trying to process all that's happened. I've taken more pain meds. The doctor said it wouldn't hurt the baby, but Dean isn't so sure. It's not that I don't care. I do. But everything hurts. My head. My arm. My heart.

Behind me, Dean snores softly. He kept asking me to come to bed, but I couldn't. I didn't want to lie down. Being still was torture, even with his arms around me. My thoughts were racing, making me feel like if I didn't *do* something, I might lose my mind. What I did was walk to the window and open the curtains. What I did was stare and stare and stare.

Mom almost aborted me. Or maybe she didn't. What if she just said that to Andy Asshole so he would never look for her, never come near her, near *us*, again? What if she thought he would hurt me, so she lied to him? That's a possibility, right? But the curandera said she was going to put me up for adoption. So she was confused, like I am. That much is certainly true.

I lift Mom's necklace and stare at the sun pendant, hearing Mom in the white light saying, "'It is the east, and Juliet is the sun.'" Whatever she was going to do with me in the beginning, one thing is undeniable. She fucking loved me. I know it. I know it because every day, every night, she was there beside me, telling me so. I know because that time a dog bit me, she wanted to kill it. I know because she read me bedtime stories and played Monopoly with me and taught me to drive. I know because even after she died, she somehow managed to show me she was still there. She loved me so much, death wasn't strong enough to keep her from me. Andy Asshole said Mom was the great love of his life, but he was wrong. Mom was the great love of mine. That's the one thing I am sure of.

NINETEEN

We order room service for breakfast. Dean gets an omelet. I order waffles. We sit on the unmade bed with trays in front of us, feeling like royalty. Dean gets my coffee ready for me, three creams, two sugars, the way I like it. He cuts up the waffle because he knows it will be hard for me to do with the cast. Then he switches on the TV. "What do you want to watch?" he asks.

"Go to the Spanish channel," I say.

He does. One of the soap operas Mom and I used to love is on. Two scantily clad women are fighting in a kitchen, screaming at each other.

"You bitch!" I put English words in their mouths, like Mom and I would have done. "You ate my Wheat Thins."

Without missing a beat, Dean jumps in. "I was hungry, you whore. And last week, you ate all of my flan. So now we're even."

One of the women picks up a knife. "You will pay!" I say. "With your life."

The other woman grabs the knifer by the arm.

Dean says, "Wait. Let's make up. Hold my hand."

The woman swings her knife.

"No," I say. "I will never forgive you for what you have done. Some debts can only be repaid in blood."

We laugh, and then Dean asks, "Do you know where you want to go today?"

I nod. I thought about it all night. "New York." As soon as I say it, I'm scared. Because it's real. There was a reason Mom's ashes sat on that countertop for so long. I couldn't let them go. I wasn't ready to say goodbye to her. But Mom's not in her ashes. I know that now. She's out there somewhere, floating in white light.

~~

We drive all day, then sleep one more night in a shitty motel, this time in Ohio. Dean wants to visit the Rock and Roll Hall of Fame. Normally, I'd be down with it, but now that I've made up my mind that I'm ready to go home, I don't want to waste any more time. So we spend another day driving, lost in our thoughts, barely talking, just liking the idea of being together, touching each other's skin, feeling the wind on our faces. It's midnight when we get to New York. The sensation of coming home is palpable. Everything smells gritty and alive, dirty, the way the world is supposed to smell. The blazing lights of the city throb in time to the pounding of my blood. The honking taxis sound like music. The drunk, homeless men huddled on the street corners look like fallen gods.

We drive over the Brooklyn Bridge. For a moment, I watch moonlight glitter on the surface of the water, and then, I close my eyes and make a wish, like Mom and I used to do when we drove over bridges or through tunnels. I wish for Mom to be okay, wherever she is. I wish for her to know I love her. I wish for her to understand how sorry I am for leaving that candle burning. I wish that I would have sat up as she walked out of my room and said, "I love you too, Mom."

Dean rolls down his window, and warm air whooshes over my skin. My phone's GPS guides us toward the beach where Mom and I used to play, and I listen to its voice, pronouncing the names of familiar streets in its mechanized cadence. This whole city feels like Mom. We pass the vegan place where she told me about fat eyes. We pass the school where she kissed me goodbye every day when I was little. We pass the funeral home where her friends and family gathered to say goodbye to her. I didn't say goodbye that day though. I barely remember it. It's nothing but a black blur.

Memories of Mom roll over me like waves. Every one hurts. Every one is precious. I want the pain to go. I don't want to be eviscerated anymore. At the same time, I never want it to stop because this pain is my proof she existed. It's my proof that I loved her so much, she became a physical part of my being. The vacant place she left inside me is proof she was there.

As Dean pulls into the parking lot by the beach where Mom and I used to go, I put my hand out the window and reach toward the light of the moon, wondering if that's where she is now, swimming in its glow. It's redundant for me to tell you I'm crying. Of course I am. I always cry now. Before she died, never. Now? Always.

We take off our shoes when we hit the sand, and Dean puts his arm around my waist. My saddlebag weighs me down. I have removed everything but Mom's ashes, and still, it's heavy. Ahead, the waves roll in, crashing, calling my name. I see the place where Mom and I built a sand mermaid once, remembering her seashell eyes and seaweed hair. I picture Mom sitting on that jagged rock, calling me the sun. When I reach the water's edge, I kneel, never mind my clothes. Let them get wet. Let them be stained. Let them be wrecked. Let them drink in the salt of the ocean and be forever changed by this moment.

I unzip the saddlebag and reach inside, rubbing the silt of Mom's ashes between my fingers, feeling the tiny shards left of her bones. I read once that the author Cheryl Strayed ate her mother's ashes, and I understand the impulse. I want to ingest her, not let her go. But I have to let her go. I have to let her go because she's already gone.

I open the saddlebag and pour its contents onto the surface of the hungry sea, watching them dance there for a moment, glittering white in the moonlight. "'But soft, what light from yonder window breaks?'" I whisper. "It is the east, and Mary is the moon." I feel it as I say it, Mom as big as the sky, flying free. She doesn't live in this saddlebag. She never did. She's out there somewhere, and she isn't screaming anymore. Somewhere, Mom is dancing.

I send Mom away with a song, wanting to give her music to sway to, wherever she is.

I close my eyes as I sing, and when I open my eyes, the ashes have disappeared.

TWENTY

I don't know why Dean and I haven't had sex since he came back to me. Maybe it's my arm. Maybe it's my heart. But as much as the sight of him makes my belly flip-flop, something in me isn't quite ready for it. Dean never pushes. At night, we sleep in shitty motel rooms, and he holds my head against his chest, letting me soak his shirt with my tears. I play with his crucifix, touch his mouth, and study the many different shades of blue woven into the webs of his irises. When he sleeps, I run my finger over the lettering of his "unbroken" tattoo, wondering if someday I will feel like that. Right now, I'm shattered.

Still, I'm starting to mend. The sensation is palpable. I can almost see my soul knitting itself back together, just as my arm bones are. I let myself be close to Dean, beating back the Harley who believed she could never love again, telling her it's time for her to stop ruining my life. Not that

I'm an utterly changed woman. My propensity for posturing, as Dean called it, still comes out some days. I snap at him, say hurtful things, and pull away when he needs to talk. But somehow, he always forgives me, and as the days go by, I find myself doing these things less and less. I start to think Dean is my proof that something up there, Mom or god or Yoda, is watching out for me. How else would he have found me under that dock?

During the days, we drive back toward California, more or less, meandering through America, stopping along the way to see sites. We see the sun rise over Ellis Island and watch rainbows ricochet from crashing torrents at Niagara Falls. We visit Dollywood and the Johnny Cash Museum and the Rock and Roll Hall of Fame, spending a few days in each city we land in, trying to make the most of it, take it all in. When we get back to Nebraska, we stop at Three Guys Body Shop, which is as titillating as its name lets on. The postage-stamp-size garage cannot be accused of false advertising. There are indeed three guys inside, all white, pudgy, and smudged with grease. But I barely notice them. What I see is my Harley sitting in the corner of the parking lot, wedged between an SUV and a Prius, shining like a million suns.

"That's the only thing in this world I love more than you," I tell Dean, walking toward the window to get a closer look.

"Uh-oh." Dean smiles. "Are you going to leave me for a motorcycle?"

"Sometimes," I say. "But I'll always come back."

He comes to me and kisses my forehead. "Deal."

We tie up the bike in the back of Dean's truck and drive away. I can't stop looking through the window, watching her. "Fuck this broken arm," I say. "I want to ride."

"Fuck that broken arm," Dean says. He turns up the radio, and together, we sing with Modest Mouse. I think they're right. We will float on.

When the song fades into commercials, Dean switches the radio off.

"Would you think I was crazy if I told you I want to call my dad again?" I ask.

He smiles. "I'd think you were crazy if you didn't."

"I mean, he spent eighteen years trying to make up for what he did to Mom."

"I had an uncle who was an alcoholic," Dean says. "He couldn't stay sober for a month. Staying sober for two decades takes a lot of strength. The illustrious Mr. Warphol can't be all bad."

I nod. "The least I can do is give him a chance."

"You don't have to convince me." Momentarily, Dean lifts his hands from the wheel in a surrender motion.

"And he seemed pretty nice, if you can get around the fact that he punched my mom once upon a time." I'm trying to persuade myself, not Dean. I've been thinking a lot about my dad since that day in the studio. I'm still pissed, but it seems wasteful not to utilize the only parental unit I have left.

Dean drapes his arm over me. "His paintings were a little weird."

"Good weird?" I ask.

"If you think freakish, postapocalyptic zombie-death-creatures are good."

"You know I do."

"Me too. They're my favorite kind of people." He kisses the top of my head. "That's why I'm dating you."

I smack him with my good arm.

⁓ℰ⌒

A few weeks later, I stand beside the Grand Canyon for the first time. Grasping Dean's hand in wonder and fear, I feel the smallness of me and the greatness of all that is. I drink in the colors below us—the rusty, jagged rocks, the emerald trees, and the turquoise snake of a river. For a moment, I'm genuinely happy. I forget to hurt.

As the sun melts into the horizon, painting the canyon with blazing crimson, Dean and I sit on the edge of a cliff, our feet dangling over the edge. The floor is forever away, and I shiver at the thought of falling. I move closer to Dean, who pours sparkling cider into plastic glasses. I wish it was champagne, but I can't have that when I'm pregnant, and neither of us is old enough to buy it anyway.

"How's our girl?" he asks me, pressing a glass into my hand and touching the tiny bump of my belly.

I smile. "I think she's okay." I lean against him, wincing at the jolt of dull pain that shoots through my collarbone. I don't take the prescription meds anymore, just Tylenol, which means I have to feel the pain in my body as well as my heart, but I guess that's part of life. I've figured out that soul wounds are like physical wounds. You have to let them ache when they want to. They will throb until they scab over and form a scar. They will hurt until they don't. So when the grief comes, I let it wash over me, reminding myself that it's only pain, that I have survived worse than this.

Watching the edges of clouds go fuchsia, I think about my baby, trying to process the fact that there are tiny toes and fingers growing inside me. I try to imagine what it would be like to give her to someone else, someone better equipped to raise her. It breaks me.

"Whether we decide to raise her or not, I want to call her Mary," I say.

He bends to kiss our baby. "Hello, in there, Mary." He whispers into my belly button like it is some biologically engineered microphone.

Together, we lift our glasses toward the setting sun. "To Mary," I say, watching birds volcano from trees, blurring the horizon with red-winged visions.

Sipping cider, we gaze out at the canyon in silence until purple twilight. "I want to do what's best for her," I say as the first stars appear. "That's all I care about."

That night, we stay at a hotel in nearby Flagstaff. It's a funky college town nestled in blue mountains. Its people are kind, not like New Yorkers, and down to earth, not like Californians. They wear hiking boots instead of high heels. If you ask them for directions, they smile and point the way.

"I like this place," I say to Dean as we flop onto the hotel bed.

"Me too," he says. "Maybe I could go to college here. I hear they have a killer creative writing program."

When I stopped pushing Dean away, I learned that his poems weren't just a hobby. He wants to go pro.

"I'd miss you," I say.

"You could move here with me."

I glance at him, trying to figure out if he's serious. He is. I'm shocked that the idea of living here with him, maybe in one of those adobe houses we saw as we drove in, doesn't terrify me. Still, I'm not quite ready to have that conversation. I change the subject. "Should we order room service?"

"I don't know," Dean says. "Maybe we should go to the restaurant downstairs. I'm tired of being cooped up. The sign in the lobby said there's a band playing tonight."

I can't imagine what kind of band would be playing in a hotel lobby in Flagstaff, but Dean's right. Being stuck in hotel rooms is getting old. "I'm game."

Half an hour later, we sit at a table in a tiny restaurant, quartered off from the rest of the hotel by a low wall and frosted glass. A small stage sits in the corner, encircled by a wooden dance floor. A bar rests at the center, its TVs blaring some game or another. Hockey? Soccer? Football? It's all the same to me.

"Do you want to split the steak?" Dean asks. Recently, we have begun to share meals. I say it's because it saves money, but really, it's because it makes me feel closer to Dean.

"Sure," I say.

"How do you want it cooked?" he asks.

"Medium," I say.

Dean looks horrified. "Oh, man. I can't do that. It's a waste of a good steak. Might as well throw it straight into a fire and eat the ashes."

"Normally, I'd agree, but rare meat is bad for the baby. It said so in the pamphlets the doctor gave me," I say.

"Medium it is," he says.

Dinner is way better than the atmosphere gave us a right to expect. Mom would be unhappy with my choice of red meat, but man, does it taste like heaven. And I'm pretty sure that baked potatoes with sour cream slathered on top are the food of the gods. Fuck ambrosia.

"Am I putting on weight?" I ask Dean through a mouthful of butter-soaked veggies.

"Not at all," he says, but I can see in his eyes he's lying.

"I am!" I say excitedly. I've been trying to gain weight for years, and now, my magic baby is making it happen. "Don't worry. It's a good thing! For the record, when it comes to me, the correct answer to the question, 'Does my ass look fat in these jeans?' is always yes."

Dean laughs. "Okay then. You look resplendently voluptuous!"

"Go me!" I say, raising my fist in victory.

After we eat, Dean orders a beer, and they give it to him without carding him. As the waitress sets it in front of him, we exchange glances, sharing that secret thrill that comes from getting one over on the proverbial man.

"Today, we pull off underage drinking. Tomorrow, we take over the world," I whisper as the waitress walks away.

Dean grins. When he kisses me, his mouth tastes like beer. I want one so bad, but I'm not going to make the same mistake twice. Instead, I sip my Sprite as the band takes the stage.

The band is not quite what I expected. It consists of four gray-haired men, all of them close to seventy. They wear Hawaiian shirts, jeans, and really bad hats, probably to cover bald spots. "Uh-oh," I say to Dean. "Get ready to hear some golden oldies."

"Hello, Flagstaff!" the lead singer yells, as if he is Mick Jagger greeting an arena full of screaming fans. "Let's rock!" As the band launches into a surprisingly competent rendition of "Mustang Sally," I look around the room and realize every other person here is a senior citizen. I shout to Dean to be heard over the music. "I think we just landed in Old People Oz!" Clearly, this geriatric concert is some weekly Flagstaff senior citizen tradition. Everyone seems to know everyone else.

Dean shouts back, "I hope I'm this cool when I'm old."

The band plays song after song, some of them classic, some of them not. All of them are awesome. Old ladies line dance, their garishly dyed heads and sagging breasts bouncing in time to the music. At first, I think they're funny. Then, I start to think they are the most beautiful women I've ever seen. They are what I want to be when I grow up. Hell, they are what I want to be now.

"That's what freedom looks like," I tell Dean. Even though I'm not drinking, I start to feel drunk. Dean *is* drinking, and judging by the way he keeps fondling me under the table, he *is* drunk. I don't mind. I like when Dean touches me.

An old woman approaches. She has cat-eye glasses and blue streaks in her hair. I want to tell Dean she gives a whole new meaning to blue-haired lady, but I can't because she's standing right there. "You kids need to come dance!"

Instantly, my buzz is gone. "No, thanks," I say. No way am I dancing in public. No. Way.

Smiling, the woman tosses her head. "Suit yourself," she says, walking away.

"Come on, Harley." Dean stands and takes my hand. "Let's dance."

"You go," I say. "I'll watch."

Dean kisses me and then joins the revelry. I watch him and the old ladies sway and bop to "Achy Breaky Heart." I study their feet, thinking maybe when I'm alone, I will practice these moves so next time I get the chance, I can dance.

Dean returns to me breathless and smiling. "What a rush!" he says. He waves the waitress down and orders another beer. As he takes his first sip, the band begins a familiar song. I can't place right it right away, but after a few chords, I know. It's Mom's Jean-Luc Picard song, the one I thought only she knew. When the singer starts the first verse, I think I'm going to burst into tears, but instead, I start to laugh.

"What?" Dean shouts. "What's so funny?"

"She's here!" I say. "This is how she talks to me now. Through music. My mom is here!" Warm emotion wraps around me, just like it did that day in the white light. I know

I'm not alone. I know there is magic in this world. I yank Dean's face close and kiss him hard. His mouth still tastes like beer. I drink him down.

"Wanna go upstairs?" he asks. I do, but I don't. Somehow, this old people fest has turned into the most exhilarating experience of my life. I want to see it through to its end. The band keeps playing. "Honky Tonk Woman." "Bad Romance." "Heartbreak Hotel." The old ladies keep drinking wine and dancing. I memorize their moves. Their steps become clumsier, but their faces shine. And then, the lead singer says, "And now, I'm going to give the microphone to an old friend of mine, one of the most captivating women I've ever known. We played in a band together when we were young, and she's passing through town. Ladies and gentlemen, please welcome Jean Whittler." I don't recognize her name, but as soon as she steps onto the stage, I know her. She's wearing a push-up bra and a zebra-striped shirt. Her red hair gleams, as if she just touched it up. Before, I thought maybe she was a kind of beautiful I couldn't see. Now, I see it.

I grab Dean's hand. "Oh my god! I know her!"

"No way!" Dean says.

"Yeah," I shout. "I met her at a campground. She's awesome!"

Smiling, Jean takes the microphone from the stand and starts to sway and sing "Girl Crush." She has the most glorious voice I've ever heard. You'd never know by listening that she's a day over thirty.

When she's done, applause erupts. Old men hoot and

holler as she leaves the stage, as if she is Beyoncé. I run to her
and throw my arms around her.

"Harley!" she says. "What the hell are you doing here?"

"I'm on my way home!" I shout as the band starts to play
"Friends in Low Places."

"You spread your mom's ashes?" she asks.

I nod.

She pats my cheek. "Then the hard part is over. Time
to cut loose." She grabs my hand and pulls me toward the
dance floor.

"No! I don't dance!" I say, but she either doesn't hear
me, or she doesn't care.

And then, here I am, in the line, and I have two choices.
I can either stand around like an asshole, or I can dance. I
dance, tentatively at first, watching the disco balls shatter light
over the wooden slats of the dance floor, thinking hard about
what my feet are doing, making sure I get the steps right.
When I glance at Jean, her head is thrown back in ecstasy. She
looks like she won a million dollars or shot up with heroine.
I want to be like her. I want to be free and happy and forever
young. So I let go. I throw my head back too, smile, and let
the music wash over me, the way I have been letting the pain
wash over me when it comes. The drumbeats move my feet,
and suddenly, I'm not afraid anymore, not of dancing, but of
anything. I feel like the world is mine.

"You have badass moves!" I hear Dean say. I turn, and
he's behind me, moving with the line.

"This is the best night of my whole life!" I shout.

We finish the dance, and then, I kiss him hard. His heat fills me. I want him more than anything in the world, and I'm not scared of it anymore.

When the show is over, we make plans to meet Jean and Lawrence for breakfast. Then we go back to our room. I can't get Dean's clothes off fast enough. No, that isn't an expression. Have you ever tried undressing someone with one arm? It's fucking hard. But with Dean's help, I get the job done. Then, the world stops. As I look into his eyes, I see the sky in them, thinking that maybe, just maybe, Mom was right.

Maybe the part of us that matters goes on forever.

EPILOGUE

They tell you labor hurts, and you think you get what they mean, but you don't. It feels like somebody is stirring your guts with a machete. It's like dying. The pain makes you forget who you are. You become something bigger than self. You become a life giver.

As I push you from my body, the lights swirl, the way they must have swirled for my mom as she passed from this world into the next. I tell myself I won't scream, but I do, and then, the doctor holds you, naked and bloody and white. Your tiny mouth forms a perfect "o," and you gasp your very first breath. As you start to wail, all the agony becomes worth it because I love you more than I ever thought I could love anything.

"It's a healthy baby girl," says the doctor. Standing on the left side of my bed, Dean and Mercy start to laugh, just the way my old friend Amy said you do when your world is coming to an end. My world is ending and beginning all at the same time so I laugh too. The doctor places you on my belly.

"'But soft, what light from yonder window breaks?'" I whisper, and your crying slows, stops altogether. I look into your eyes, pale blue, and I see forever in them, the way I see forever when I look into the sea. Tentatively, I touch the miracle of your perfect ear. "It is the east, and Mary is the moon."

Your parents are standing on the right side of the bed crying. Crying for the joy of your existence. Crying for the miracle of you. They all are, everyone but me. Your dad is tall and strong, the kind of dad I always wished I'd had. Your mom is pretty and blond. You won't believe this, but she looks a lot like my mom.

"Hi, Mary," says your dad. His voice when he says your name sounds the way my mom's sounded when I met her after my wreck. It sounds like love incarnated as sound waves. I start to cry too, because I've been crying for months now. Why break tradition? You gaze at me, and I see that light in your eyes, the liquid kind I saw when Mom came to me. I know she's here with us, somehow, just like Jean said she would be. And I know I will love you forever, even if I never see you again in this world. But still, I pray I will.

My baby, I don't know if god has a name. I don't know what happens when we die. But I do know for sure there is a heaven because I see it in your eyes. And looking into your face, I know that this love flowing from me to you and back again, is the same love my mom passed on to me when she first held me. It's too powerful to die. It's just like she said. I find my home when your tiny hand wraps around my finger.

I pull you to me and kiss the top of your head, crying because my heart's breaking, because I know this is the last time I will kiss you, maybe in forever, unless you read this letter when you are eighteen and decide you want to find me. If you don't, I understand, but I never wanted you to question if you were loved by your birth parents. Because you were. You are. I can promise you that every day between now and the day I see you again, whether it is in this world or the next, I will be whispering your name, a prayer, a mantra, a hymn.

Your parents lean over me, touching your face, still crying at the wonder of you, ready to take you to the place that you will call home, and even though I want more than anything to hold you always, I let you go because I know this is what love does. It does the thing that is best for the other, not the thing that is best for the self.

I will carry the home I found in your eyes close to my heart forever.

When I press this letter into your mom's hands, I will ask her to give it to you when you are eighteen. I told you the whole truth. Lies don't serve anyone. I learned that when I met my dad. I called him again right before you were born. He flew to California to see me, carrying his painting of Mom. It hangs in my bedroom now. I imagine it will hang in the house me and Dean will be renting in Flagstaff when we move there to start college next month. The painting is weird, but so is my dad. I like it. I like him. He'll never be what Mom was to me, but he's something.

I didn't leave the "fucks" out of my story because my mom never left them out for me, and it only made me love her more. There is something beautiful in our humanity, even the fucked-up pieces of it. Especially the fucked-up pieces of it. You will find a necklace inside this envelope. It belonged to my mother, the most beautiful woman I have ever known, and then it belonged to me. Now it belongs to you, Mary. Your parents promised to use the name I chose for you. So these are my gifts to you: this letter, my necklace, and your name, a name that belonged to my mother, the most amazing woman I have ever known. A name that belongs to that stone goddess that spoke to me from her sacred cove in Omaha. A name that now belongs to you, the greatest love of my life.

My baby, think of me when you look at the sea. Think of the way life is like the waves, crashing and changing form always, but never stopping. Think of the miracles swimming under the water, manta rays and whales and schools of fish scattering light like disco balls. Nothing lasts forever, but everything never ends.

My baby, my love, my home, my sun—go into this world and live.

ACKNOWLEDGMENTS

Thank you to:

My Creator, in each of your many guises, you take my breath away. May my words give voice to your light.

The great love of my life, my Shining One, I said I'd love you forever, and I meant it. There is a piece of you in every word I write.

My best friends and precious children, Desi and Tim, this book was inspired by my love for you. You astonish me every day with your brilliance, kindness, and beauty. Also, you make me laugh hella hard. And both of you have fat eyes.

My incredible parents, Christine and Tim, you set the bar high by being two of the most magnificent people I've ever known. I'm honored to carry your blood in my veins and your love in my heart. (Daddy, it wasn't until I was three-quarters through this book I realized I was writing about my grief at your passing. It took me twenty-two years to find the words to say goodbye. I'm a little slow on the uptake. Thank you for teaching me that love is stronger than death.)

My big brother Bryan, you think you've lost your light, but you're blazing more brilliantly than ever before, inspiring everyone you touch, especially me. Blaze on.

My soul sister Polyxeni, I didn't have an army of angels. I had just a handful, and you were one of the bravest. Our ragtag band of misfits was more than enough. Thank you for saving my life a bazillion times.

My dear friend, greatest champion, and wonderful agent, Andy Ross, who guided the creation of this book from word one to publication (and who also does a mean Hamlet impression).

My fearless partner-in-San-Miguelian-crime, co-drive-by-carroter, and infinitely patient salsa dance teacher, Ashlynne Dumbledore Presley, who made my life a whole lot less lonely during one of its darkest nights. I love you, Ash.

My amazing editor Annette Pollert-Morgan, who makes my books a billion times more beautiful than they would be without her brilliance. I am so grateful for the privilege of working with you again.

Cassie Gutman, whose careful line edits contributed so much to this work.

Kerri Resnick and Nicole Hower, for embodying Harley's spirit in your masterful cover design. I couldn't love it any more than I do.

And the entire creative team at Sourcebooks Fire. I'm honored to be a part of your breathtaking artistic vision.

ABOUT THE AUTHOR

Tawni Waters is the author of the novel *Beauty of the Broken*, which won multiple awards including an International Literary Association (ILA) award, and a collection of poems, *Siren Song*. Her work has been widely published in journals, anthologies, and magazines. She teaches creative writing at various universities, conferences, and retreats throughout the United States, Europe, and Mexico. Visit her at tawniwaters.com or follow her on Facebook at facebook.com/tawniveewaters/.